"There is something about this mummy in particular that makes me fear the worst. Look at this. . . ."

Churchill knelt on the floor beside the mummy. "The heart should be beside the mummy, right?"

"Yes," Alex answered.

"Would you take a look at it?"

Alex put his hand inside the mummy's chest and touched something hard and dry—the shrunken heart.

As he pulled it out, the two-thousand-year-old heart expanded rapidly, then contracted. The heart was still beating!

The pallbearers gasped.

Suddenly, the mummy reached up, grabbed Alex's wrist, and roared.

Don't miss any thrilling

MUMMY
CHRONICLES

featuring Alex O'Connell

Book I: *Revenge of the Scorpion King*

Coming soon:

Book III: *The Curse of the Nile*

Book IV: *Flight of the Phoenix*

THE MUMMY CHRONICLES

BOOK II

HEART OF THE PHARAOH

by Dave Wolverton

Based on the motion picture screenplay
The Mummy Returns by Stephen Sommers

BANTAM BOOKS

NEW YORK · TORONTO · LONDON · SYDNEY · AUCKLAND

THE MUMMY RETURNS.

RL 5.0, AGES 009–012

HEART OF THE PHARAOH

A Bantam Skylark Book / June 2001

ISBN: 0-553-48755-8

Visit us on the Web! www.randomhouse.com/kids

**Educators and librarians, for a variety of teaching tools, visit us at
www.randomhouse.com/teachers**

Published simultaneously in the United States and Canada

BANTAM SKYLARK is an imprint of Random House Children's Books, a division of
Random House, Inc. SKYLARK BOOK and colophon and BANTAM BOOKS and colophon
are registered trademarks of Random House, Inc. Bantam Books, 1540 Broadway,
New York, New York 10036.

PRINTED IN THE UNITED STATES OF AMERICA

OPM 10 9 8 7 6 5 4 3 2 1

CONTENTS

Prologue
TOMBS AND CURSES

EGYPT—31 B.C.

There were mummies hidden in the walls of Cleopatra's tomb. They crept through secret passages, laughing eerily through rotting mouths.

Roman soldiers stood in the tomb's antechamber and waited anxiously for the mummies to spring their next trap.

"Keep going!" the Roman general Octavio commanded, and charged forward.

Suddenly, a rock wall crumbled beside him, revealing a small passageway. An Egyptian priest blocked the entrance. He wore a black mask that was carved to look like a fierce jackal; a white leopard cape clung to his shoulders. A dozen mummified guards stood with swords raised behind him.

"Go back!" the priest ordered. "The pharaoh is preparing for her journey to heaven. Do not defile this sacred place!"

Mummies and a priest were no match for Rome's finest soldiers. General Octavio and his men had fought Cleopatra's armies, the armies of the richest nation in the world. He had destroyed Egypt, and if Cleopatra hadn't killed herself moments before defeat, Octavio would have taken her back to Rome as a prisoner in chains.

Octavio gritted his teeth. "Kill them all!" he shouted.

His soldiers struck the mummies with fierce swords, cleaving their papery bodies in two. The mummies roared in anger and collapsed on the floor. When the battle was done, the priest lay gasping in a pool of blood. Octavio climbed over him, gazed into Cleopatra's treasure room—and gasped.

The room was so large that he could not see the far end—only dim reflections of light.

Gold coffins and statues of Greek and Egyptian gods lined the walls. Jeweled necklaces and headdresses were heaped on the floor beside golden couches, beds, platters, and cups. There was a chariot for Cleopatra to ride in the afterlife, with life-sized horses carved of fine jasper. Behind this mountain of wealth loomed something massive.

"More light," Octavio shouted to his soldiers. "I need more light."

His men lit Egyptian torches made of papyrus dipped in beeswax. The torches glowed in the darkness like red eyes, revealing Cleopatra's treasure.

Looming above the piles of riches was an eighty-foot ship. Every inch of the ship had been covered in gold, except for its sixty oars, which were made of silver, and its sails, which were purple silk.

General Octavio stared at it greedily, then noticed that in front of the ship was a pair of golden caskets. Both were painted in the Roman style, with a portrait of the corpse on each lid. Octavio recognized his enemies immediately. "General Mark Anthony," he said through gritted teeth. Lying next to him, wearing a cobra crown, was Cleopatra.

Octavio grinned. He would take Cleopatra back to Rome after all.

"Take the caskets and the gold," he ordered his men.

"No!" an Egyptian shrieked at Octavio's back. Octavio turned. It was the spy Octavio had hired to show him the way to the tombs. The spy rushed forward with a torch and raised it to the nearest wall. Above him were Egyptian hieroglyphs, pictures of angry owls and evil eyes. In the wavering firelight, they seemed to dance in eerie patterns. "There are curses written on the walls," he warned, "powerful magic spells! They say that no man of Rome may take this treasure. To do so will bring death to the man who touches the gold, death to the lord of Rome, and the downfall of the whole nation!"

"Do you think me a fool?" Octavio argued. "Do you think I'll leave all this treasure for you?"

"No!" the spy whined. "Truly, the curse forbids it!"

Octavio looked for a soldier brave enough to touch the treasure, but his staunchest men backed away.

"If no man of Rome may take the treasure, then a man of Egypt will." Octavio glared at the spy. "Bring me the gold."

"But—" the spy began to object. Octavio swung his sword, stopping its sharp blade an inch from the spy's throat. The spy cringed and said timidly, "As you wish!"

Trembling in fear, with sweat dotting his forehead, the spy tottered toward the treasure.

The dying priest rose up on one hand, as if pleading with the spy to stop. Blood spurted from his mouth as he uttered a curse: *"Menânâ sha!"* Die, *you pig!*

The room filled with a hissing sound like a rushing wind. Before the spy could cry out, the golden cobra rose up from Cleopatra's coffin, its eyes glowing like embers. A stream of fire rushed from its fanged mouth, engulfing the poor spy. Instantly, every drop of water in him turned to steam. All that was left was a pile of burning ashes that dropped to the floor.

The heat was so intense that Octavio's men cried out in horror.

Octavio merely smiled grimly. He knew that the Egyptians believed that Cleopatra would need her ship to sail through the seas of the underworld. He would have his revenge.

"Keep your treasure then, Cleopatra. But my own curse I leave upon you: you shall be left to waste in your Egyptian hell. You shall never make your voyage to the spirit world."

He hurled a torch into the sails of Cleopatra's golden ship. Eerie wails of dismay and pain arose from hundreds of coffins in the tomb. General Octavio watched to make sure the flames engulfed the ship, then turned and strode away.

1

A STRANGER IN THE DARK

London — 1937

Thunder boomed outside twelve-year-old Alex O'Connell's home, waking him from his sleep. As it faded in the distance, he heard a steady thumping from downstairs.

Someone was pounding on the front door.

For half a moment he waited for his parents to answer, then remembered that they were gone for the evening and wouldn't be back until late.

He ran to the window and looked down. On the cobblestone lane in front of the house was a horse-drawn hearse. Two brawny men were trying to wrestle a casket out of the back.

"What the devil?" Alex mouthed. Was this some kind of joke? It was Allhallows Eve, after all, and it seemed like just the kind of prank some of his mum's students at Bembridge might pull. She had recently accepted a post at the college teaching Egyptology and had moved the family back to London, much to Alex's disappointment. He missed the warmth of Egypt, a place where the skies were more likely to drench you in warm sunlight than cold showers.

From the front door, the pounding came more fiercely. A deep-voiced man shouted, "Halloo. Anyone there? I must speak with Mr. and Mrs. O'Connell. It's the utmost emergency!"

Alex flipped a light switch but found that the power was out. He threw a bathrobe over his pajamas, rushed downstairs, and flung open the door.

A heavyset man was about to bat the door again with his mahogany walking stick. Alex cringed as it stopped inches from his face.

"So sorry, young fellow," the man said. He wore gold-rimmed spectacles that were fogged and wet, along with a gray bowler hat and cloak. "Are your parents home?"

"No," Alex said. "They went to see a play downtown."

"Oh, bother," the man sighed. "I need to get an urgent message to them."

"I can give it to them," Alex offered.

"No, no, no," the man muttered. "This is a matter of great importance . . . to all of England, I dare-say. I shan't entrust it to some woolly-headed boy. Such matters are far beyond the understanding of mere children."

Alex glowered. "Some children understand things better than most adults."

"Hah, well said!" the man replied. "Well said indeed. With retorts like that, you could go into politics." He glanced back at the hearse. The pallbearers had just pulled the casket out and were now trying to lower it to the ground. In the sitting room, the grandfather clock began to chime.

Lightning blasted a tree on the hill, and for a moment the man's face was limned in light. Alex recognized it immediately.

"Winston Churchill, from Parliament?" Alex blurted out in surprise. "Please come in. My parents would have my head if they knew I kept you waiting outside. I don't think they'll be much longer."

Churchill looked up at the pouring rain, "I don't mind if I do." He shouted to the pallbearers, "Careful with that casket."

The pallbearers grunted and panted.

Alex led Churchill to the sitting room. "I'm sorry

about the lights," Alex said. "The power must be out." The house was three hundred years old, and there were oil lamps in brackets attached to the wall. The lamps served mostly as ornaments, but now Alex took one down to light it and stared at Churchill in awe.

"I recognized your face from the Sunday *News*," Alex told him. "I listen to your speeches on the radio all the time."

"How nice," Churchill said, arching his brow as if in disbelief. "Although some don't call them speeches so much as tirades."

"Oh, but I agree entirely with your views," Alex said. "My parents and I talk about them all the time. We've been especially troubled by Hitler's recent treaty with Mussolini, where they divided the world into 'spheres of influence.' It's pretty cheeky of the Germans and Italians to split up the world before they've even conquered it, don't you think?"

Churchill laughed. "Now there's a bright lad! Perhaps I *can* trust you to deliver a message. But if I do, you must promise to give it to your parents as soon as they come home. You can't fall asleep."

"Yes, sir, Mr. Churchill."

"I've heard about your parents' exploits in Egypt," Churchill said. "All that business about fighting mummies. Your mum is a daring Egyptologist, and your father is quite an adventurer. They're just the kind of people I need."

Alex smiled with pride. Four years ago, his parents had saved him—and the world—from two cursed creatures, Imhotep and the Scorpion King. It had been his parents' second encounter with Imhotep, and they'd barely made it home alive.

"What's happened now?" Alex asked.

"Early this morning we got word from the government of Egypt," Churchill replied. "It seems that Mussolini has sent an expedition to search for tombs in ancient Egypt. Ever since King Tutankhamen's tomb was discovered, Mussolini's been convinced that the ancient pharaohs had a nearly inexhaustible supply of gold—gold that he could use to buy tanks."

"My mum says Tutankhamen's tomb was one of the greatest discoveries in archaeological history," Alex replied, "but the tombs have more than just gold in them. They are guarded by powerful spells."

Thunder shook the house, rattling the windows and lamps. Churchill clutched his hat tightly as Alex continued.

"When we lived in Egypt, I was training to be a Medjai, like my friend Ardeth Bay. He's their leader. The Medjai protect the tombs from foolish intruders and try to keep ancient forces locked inside where they belong." Alex paused and stepped closer to Churchill. "But some creatures are too powerful to control. Before I left Egypt, the Scorpion King rose from the dead again. If it wasn't for the Medjai, the Scorpion King and his warriors would have killed my friend and me!"

"Wow," Churchill said with a shudder. "Until a few hours ago, I'd always believed that all this talk about Egyptian curses was a bunch of nonsensical hocus-pocus. Now an object has come into my possession . . ." He nodded toward the door just as the pallbearers wrestled the wet coffin inside.

One of the men slipped, and the casket spilled open. A gruesome mummy rolled onto the floor!

2

THE MUMMY'S HEART

"**B**limey," one pallbearer said as he stared at the mummy in its gray bandages. Half of its face had rotted away. "I wouldn't kiss that thing on a dare."

The roots of the mummy's yellow teeth were exposed where the lips and cheek had decayed. Alex glanced at it and shrugged. He had seen worse.

"This mummy was intercepted at the docks in Cairo," Churchill said. "It was headed for Italy. It appears that a team of treasure hunters has made a find, possibly a very valuable one. I was hoping that your mother might be able to identify the location of the site from the casket."

"Mind if I take a look?" Alex asked. "My mum's been teaching me about mummies since before I could read." He carried the oil lamp to the coffin. It was covered with soot and dust. "This has been in a fire," he told them. Gently he began to brush off the soot. He could see some faded paint beneath it.

"There's a picture on here," Alex said. "Rich Greeks and Romans always had their portraits painted on their caskets. That means this is a recent burial as far as mummies go, probably some time after the Romans took over Egypt."

He rubbed away the dust to reveal the face of a young servant girl, perhaps fourteen—only two years older than Alex. She had dark, flowing hair and a small, sad smile. Her eyes were large and haunting, as if she were waiting for something that would never come.

"She died so young," Alex said. A wave of pity swept through him. The girl had probably let herself be sacrificed when her pharaoh died, so that she could escort her lord to heaven.

The pallbearer took off his hat and wiped sweat from his brow. "She was a real looker once—but she's seen better days."

Alex turned his attention to the mummy on the floor. "My mum told me it used to take up to three months for the priests of Anubis to mummify people in their temple. Hundreds of dead people were often stored in there at once. The priests kept each person tagged so there were no mix-ups."

Alex felt around the bandages at the mummy's throat. "Her tag must be in here somewhere."

"Unless she's someone you've heard of before, what help will her name give us?" Churchill asked.

"The name tag will probably tell us her occupation, the year of her death, and the name of the pharaoh she served."

He felt under the bandages by the girl's throat and pulled out her rotted tag. The faded brown letters were Coptic characters, a shorthand version of Egyptian hieroglyphics. Alex wasn't very good at reading Coptic. His mouth went dry with anticipation. Outside, thunder roared in the distance.

"Her name was Irani," Alex said slowly as he translated the characters into sounds. "She was a court magician—in the palace of Queen Cleopatra!"

"Cleopatra, now that's a familiar name," Churchill said. "As I recall, she was one of the wealthiest queens of Egypt, wasn't she?"

Alex's heart was hammering. "Not one of," he said. "Of all the pharaohs, she was the richest!"

"How rich?" Churchill asked tensely.

"Compared to her, King Tut was a pauper," Alex replied. "She had the largest fleet in the world and armies to match. For years people have been scouring Egypt, looking for signs of her. This will be the find of the century!"

"Well," one of the pallbearers said, "I'll be!"

"I read a story in one of my mum's books about how Cleopatra met Mark Anthony, the head general of the Roman legions," Alex continued. "He sent letters asking to meet her while he was visiting Egypt, but she refused. She didn't want him to think he could order her around. Instead, she waited until he was giving a speech in the town square, then floated down the Nile in a boat that was covered in gold leaf. The sails were spun from purple silk, and the oars were made of silver."

"Lovely," one pallbearer sighed, staring into space.

Alex grinned. "Even the oarsmen had been painted gold, and musicians played golden flutes, harps, and drums. That's how rich she was!" he proclaimed.

Churchill furrowed his brow and muttered, "Exactly what I was afraid of . . ."

"Mark Anthony fell in love with her instantly and never willingly left her side," Alex added.

"Wasn't there a bit of trouble before this fellow?" Churchill asked.

"Yes, she was also married to Julius Caesar, the leader of the Roman Senate. The book said Caesar left his first wife to live with Cleopatra in Egypt— and caused quite a scandal in Rome."

"Of course," Churchill replied. "You can't have the leader of the senate just running off for love! Nothing would ever get done."

Alex nodded. "The Romans believed that Cleopatra was a witch who had used black magic to steal Caesar's heart. When he returned to Rome several years later, his fellow senators stabbed him in the back."

"That's when Cleopatra returned to Egypt and met Mark Anthony," Churchill concluded, stroking his chin thoughtfully.

"Exactly," Alex said. "When Mark Anthony fell in love with her, too, rumors about Cleopatra's power grew in Rome again. Caesar's brother-in-law, General Octavio, was sent to Egypt to hunt her down."

"I remember this part," Churchill said. "When

the Romans cornered her, Cleopatra decided to commit suicide."

"That's where most of the history books end," Alex said, "but Ardeth Bay told me more. He said Cleopatra built her tomb far out in Desh-Ret, the dead lands of the Sahara. The priests and sorcerers who served in her court bound the tomb with such powerful curses that no one could rob it—until at last the sands blew over the tomb and it was lost forever."

"Not forever, it seems," Churchill said. "Egypt has been plagued by fierce sandstorms for the past month. Last week, a caravan of traders took shelter in their tents behind an enormous hill of sand near an excavation site. In the morning when they woke, the hilltop was gone—revealing the jagged top of a temple. This mummy was recovered from the tomb—along with a small fortune in gold. If the reports are true, the tomb may hold more gold than all the treasuries of Europe."

Alex shook his head in disbelief as rain continued to patter on the roof.

Churchill sighed, then continued. "The Italians were the first to learn of the find. They've taken control of the tomb. In the spirit of their new alliance with Germany, Mussolini has hired a ruthless chap to lead their group, a German archaeologist named Zorin Ungricht."

Alex's blood went cold. "Ungricht tried to kill my friend and me at the Scorpion King's temple. He'll do anything for money!"

"I'll be honest," Churchill said. "If Mussolini gets his hands on that gold, he could start a real row. But I'm afraid there is a greater danger—from the mummies themselves. They are evil, unnatural creatures, aren't they?"

"Not all of them," Alex said. "Evil people make evil mummies, but good people make good mummies. It's like the Medjai taught me: Power is neither good nor evil, it's how we use it that matters."

"I agree," Churchill replied, "but there is something about this mummy in particular that makes me fear the worst. Look at this. . . ."

Churchill knelt on the floor beside the mummy. "I'm not an expert like your mum, but I know that all internal organs were removed when a person was mummified."

Alex nodded. "All the organs were taken out but

one—the heart. The Egyptians believed that the heart was weighed after death by the god Osiris to see if the good in the person's heart overbalanced the evil acts he committed."

"Indeed," Churchill said. "So the heart should be inside the mummy, right?"

"Yes," Alex answered.

"Would you take a look at it?"

Alex put his hand inside the mummy's chest and touched something hard and dry—the shrunken heart.

As he pulled it out, the two-thousand-year-old heart expanded rapidly, then contracted. The heart was still beating!

The pallbearers gasped.

Suddenly, the mummy reached up, grabbed Alex's wrist, and roared.

3
TERROR AND MAGIC

Alex ripped his arm free and bounded across the room.

The mummy cried out in a pleading voice, "*S-mam, nuk shua, h_-t p ånq! H_-t p ånq!*"

The pallbearers screamed in terror and sprinted out the door.

Churchill lunged backward, reached into the pocket of his cloak, and pulled out an enormous revolver. He fired. The first shot went over the head of the mummy and struck Alex's mother's favorite vase.

The second shot hit the mummy in the chest, throwing it backward.

Alex tried to understand the mummy's words. His mum had taught him ancient Egyptian, but the mummy's voice was difficult to make out. "Please, I beg you," she seemed to say, "return my heart!"

Alex held the beating heart in his hand and looked at the mummy. He recalled the face of the young girl on the coffin. This was no monster, no creature of darkness. She had been a person once. Her name was Irani.

"Stop!" Alex shouted at Churchill.

Churchill's face was a mask of fear. He raised the revolver and aimed it right between Irani's eyes.

"No!" Alex knocked the gun away and shouted, *"Irani, shti tuan ånq." Take back your heart.*

The mummy grabbed the heart from Alex, then fell to the floor.

Churchill's hand was trembling, and he kept gasping. He looked at Alex, then back at the mummy, then at Alex again. "By Jove," he said in awe. "How did you do that?"

4

PROMISES MADE

"I just spoke to her in ancient Egyptian," Alex explained. "I wanted to comfort her."

At that moment, Alex's father rushed into the house, shouting, "Alex, I heard shots. What the devil is going on?" He looked at the mummy on the floor and Winston Churchill standing above it.

"Mummy problems?" Alex's dad said in disgust. "Not again! I hate mummies!"

Alex's mum ran into the house behind him, glanced at the mummy, glanced at Churchill, and then stared at the remains of her favorite vase.

"What?" she asked, gathering up the pieces. "That was nearly four thousand years old! It—it graced the court of Ramses II. It withstood plundering Babylonian invaders and tomb raiders and the ten plagues of Egypt, and now—now!"

"Dreadfully sorry about the vase," Churchill blurted out. "I'll buy you another."

"Mum, Dad," Alex said. "They've found Cleopatra's tomb."

"Cleopatra?" his mum said, dropping the pieces. "Who found it?"

"Tomb raiders," Alex said. "Mussolini has sent soldiers to plunder it. Zorin Ungricht is leading them."

Alex's father's face darkened in anger.

"Oh, dear! We can't let that happen," his mum replied. "This could be the biggest archaeological find of the century! If Ungricht finds it, he'll surely melt the gold into bricks and sell anything else of value."

"You know Ungricht, too?" Churchill asked.

"Our paths have crossed before." Alex's dad lifted his shirt. Across his belly was a ragged line of old scars from gunshot wounds. "I met him at the Temple of the Monkey just outside Calcutta. I had a machete, and he had a machine gun. I lost."

"Does that mean you're not up for a trip to Cairo?" Churchill replied.

"Me?" Alex's dad scoffed. "Look, I've already

saved the world from mummies twice before. It's someone else's turn."

Alex and his mum said in unison, "Third time is the charm."

"I could cite a hundred reasons why you should go," Churchill told Alex's dad. "The Egyptian government wants to protect its antiquities but doesn't have the military might to stop the Italians. They're begging for help from the international community. The French have promised to dispatch troops from the Foreign Legion, but it will take days for them to reach the tomb from their headquarters in Algeria. The Prime Minister has given me approval to send in a small team to stop the looters. I spoke to Lord Harrill at the embassy in Egypt, and he assured me that you were the man to lead them." He counted off the reasons on his fingers. "You served extensively in the French Foreign Legion. You know the terrain. You have contacts in the area who could help you mount an expedition quickly. Besides—"

"We'll be happy to go—" Alex's mum interrupted.

"*We* will?" Alex's dad asked. "Who says *you're* going?"

"She must go," Churchill said. "Your wife is one

of the world's most reknowned Egyptologists. Obviously these mummies are unsettled. We can't run the risk that Ungricht might stir them up."

"But—"

"See here," Churchill said, "Mussolini wants to use the plunder to help finance a war, a war that will engulf all of Europe, maybe the whole world—"

"Of course we're going," Alex's mum cut in. "There's more at stake here than the war. It's our duty to preserve the integrity of the site! Besides . . ." She looked toward Irani, lying in the coffin with her beating heart in her hands. "There's something terribly wrong with this poor mummy. Obviously, she isn't quite dead. We have to help her find peace."

"She *is* a nice mummy, dad," Alex said. "When I pulled out her heart, all she did was ask for it back."

Alex's dad rolled his eyes. "If you two really want to work with dead people, maybe you should become undertakers. At least that way you can be sure your clients *stay* dead."

Alex, his mum, and Churchill all stared at Alex's dad, begging him with their eyes.

"Be a good chap," Churchill said. "Do it for England."

"Dad, please?" Alex begged. "Irani needs us."

"I've always wished I had met Cleopatra," his mum added. "Maybe we'll get lucky."

His dad shrugged. "Maybe we'll even get a new vase out of it."

Alex grinned from ear to ear. He felt as if he wasn't just going back to Egypt. He was going home!

5

SHADOWS AND SPIES

Alex and his parents sat on rickety crates in the back of a military plane to Cairo. Twenty of the grimmest soldiers Alex had ever seen sat in rows up and down both sides of the plane. Irani's casket lay in the middle.

Alex had been pestering his parents since they left the house, but they wouldn't budge. Now he turned to the soldier's leader and asked the question that was uppermost in his mind. "Captain Bronson, can I come with you to the tomb?"

"Absolutely not," Bronson said. "This is a military operation, not some field trip with your friends."

"But—" Alex began.

"Butts are for sitting on," Alex's dad said firmly, "and you'll be sitting on yours at the embassy while we go to the tomb. I thought your mother and I already made that clear."

"I want to protect the tombs, too," Alex insisted. "I can help. The Medjai taught me how—"

"Look," Bronson said. "See these twenty lads?" Alex looked at the muscular soldiers sitting around Irani's casket. "I hand-picked them. There isn't one of them who couldn't pop your head off with his bare hands and use your skull for a teacup. Maybe in another ten years you can join us—but not now."

Alex rubbed his head for a moment and considered Bronson's warning. Alarming, but he had to try. "I know some ancient Egyptian," he offered. "There are curses written on the walls of every tomb. If you open a door or touch a wall, you never know what might happen—"

"We're not afraid of curses," Bronson said impatiently.

Alex looked Bronson in the eye and very deliberately popped the lid on Irani's casket. "Are you afraid of this?" he asked, pointing to Irani's beating heart. Even the toughest of the soldiers looked nervous.

"That's enough, Alex," his mum said. "Don't frighten the soldiers. I'll be there to read the curses, and I'm sure that with your father and Captain Bronson, we're in very capable hands."

Yeah, Alex wanted to say. *Just so long as he doesn't rip your skull off and use it for a teacup.* But he knew there was no use arguing. He fell silent and resigned himself to the idea that he would have to stay away from the action. At least he'd get to see his friends, Rachel Stroeker and Matt Harrill. Matt was the son of the English ambassador, Lord Harrill. Alex and Matt had been friends since they were small. Alex had just met Rachel a few months ago. She was a German girl who had been kicked out of her homeland by the Nazis just for being Jewish. She'd helped Alex defeat the Scorpion King, and during their adventure they had become good friends.

The plane flew through most of the day, and Alex found himself thinking about Irani. *Is she scared or lonely?* he wondered. *Did she have friends like Matt or Rachel?* He wished his parents had let him bring the Medjai dagger Ardeth Bay had given him after defeating the Scorpion King. Alex shook his head and sighed. *Someday I'll be a full protector of mankind, just like Ardeth Bay. . . .*

They flew into the city at dusk, when the Muslim muezzins were out, calling the faithful to prayer. The city was awash in golden light, more light than

Alex remembered seeing for months in England. Beyond the hubbub of the markets, he could see the ancient pyramids on the horizon.

Cairo's airport was small, with only one hangar and a few planes tied to stakes. The terminal doubled as a tool-storage shed, and the dirt parking lot had more camels lying on it than cars.

The soldiers unloaded Irani's casket from the plane. Captain Bronson shook Alex's father's hand. "When do we begin?"

Alex's dad checked his watch. "We'll meet you for dinner and the debriefing at the embassy at 19:30 hours. Tell the men we'll move out from there at 21:00."

"Perfect," Captain Bronson said. He and his men left for the embassy in a waiting truck, but Alex stayed with his parents.

As they wheeled the casket across the tarmac, Alex looked to see how long his shadow was. It stretched out more than forty feet. Then he noticed something odd: there were three people in his group, but four shadows on the ground. Alex's, his mum's, his dad's . . . and behind the casket was a young woman's shadow.

"Mum, Dad," Alex said, with a shiver running down his spine. "Look!"

"Don't worry," his mum told him in a solemn tone. "It won't hurt us."

"But what is it?" Alex asked.

"The Egyptians believed that there were four eternal parts to a person," Alex's mum reminded him. "One is the *Ka*, a spirit body that looks just like your physical body. That's the part that goes to live in heaven. The other part is the *Ba*, a part of the spirit that looks like a bird. It remains on earth long enough to watch over friends and to carry messages between the worlds. The other two things that remain are the person's shadow and his name.

"Alex, do you remember what General Octavio did to Cleopatra's monuments after she died?" she asked.

Alex paused for a moment, trying to recall what he had learned. "He knocked them all down, didn't he? And had her name chiseled off every piece of stone."

"Yes," his mum said, looking thoughtfully at Irani's shadow. "He also made it illegal to even speak her name. He wanted people to forget it, so that

Cleopatra and her servants would never reach heaven."

"Is that what's wrong with Irani, Mum?" Alex asked.

"I suspect so," she answered. "No one would ever have even heard of Cleopatra if her two sons hadn't asked a scribe to write her story down."

"Now, instead of being a forgotten pharaoh, she's one of the most famous," Alex's dad added with a grin. "See, Evy, I listen."

Alex's mum rubbed his father's arm and laughed. "Sure you do."

"Don't worry, Irani," Alex whispered to the shadow in ancient Egyptian, "I'll help you find your way to the spirit world."

The shadow bowed to him, as if to say "Thank you," and stretched out a hand. With its long shadow finger, it pointed.

"What's she pointing at?" Alex's dad asked.

"Maybe she's trying to lead us somewhere," his mum replied.

The shadow began to stretch across the parking lot, becoming impossibly long. There were five cars and a few camels in the lot, along with an Arab who hunched over a motorcycle as if he was trying to fix it.

The shadow hand reached out and touched the Arab's back. He wore a long gray robe, and his kaffiyeh hid the back of his neck. It looked as if he was trying to take the engine apart with a wrench.

"She wants us to talk to that man," Alex told his parents. He took off running toward the fellow.

"*Salaam,*" Alex called in greeting, but the Arab ignored him. "*Yâ sidi?*" Sir? The fellow still didn't respond.

Maybe he doesn't hear me, Alex thought. But just as Alex drew near, the Arab suddenly stood up and threw a leg over the motorcycle. He kicked the starter, and Alex saw his face.

The fellow wasn't an Arab at all. His skin was too pale, his beard was too light, and what Alex had thought was a wrench in his hand was a pistol. Worst of all, a red-and-black Nazi emblem was painted on the motorcycle's side. He must be a German spy!

He sneered at Alex and revved the engine. Dust sprayed up from the rear wheel as he sped away.

"Dad?" Alex called.

His dad raced up beside Alex. "I saw him, too,"

his dad said. "Looks like Ungricht's men know we're here."

Alex's mum bit her lip. "Let's see about getting to the British embassy." She rushed to the airport hangar to use the phone and emerged a few minutes later.

"They'll be sending a truck to pick us up," she said, "but they have to wait for the driver to get back from another errand. He should be here in half an hour."

"Half an hour?" Alex asked. "Can I walk? It would be faster!"

His dad smiled. "Okay, but no fooling around."

Alex took off through Cairo. The vendors had closed their stalls for the evening, and hardly anyone was on the streets. The air was filled with the rich scents of people's dinners cooking—fry bread and chickpeas, lamb basted in herbs and yogurt. If Alex inhaled deeply, he thought he could even smell the desert.

Alex kept watching his feet. An extra shadow walked beside his, even though it was growing too dark to see. Somehow, he felt comforted by Irani's presence.

As he rounded a corner toward the embassy, he heard a familiar voice, calling *"BalaH! Hilu BalaH!"* *Dates for sale. Sweet dates.*

It was a common cry in the marketplace, but it wasn't common for Rachel Stroeker to be making it.

Alex looked up from the double shadows at his feet. Rachel was dressed like a traditional Egyptian girl, with a shawl wrapped over her head, and she was carrying a large platter of candied dates.

"Rach—" he began to shout, but someone grabbed his shirt collar from behind and yanked him back around the corner.

A menacing voice hissed in Arabic, "Silence, Alex O'Connell, you son of a jackal!"

6
THE CHASE

Alex craned his neck to see who had grabbed him. His attacker wore bedouin's robes and a black kaffiyeh to hide his face, but beneath the robes was a red-haired boy with freckled skin and large green eyes. It was his old friend Matthew Harrill.

"Matt?" Alex asked.

"We've been expecting you. Now please do be quiet," Matt whispered in an English accent. "Can't you see what's going on?"

"What?" Alex asked.

"You know Rachel Stroeker, right?"

"Yes," Alex said, "but I didn't know *you* knew her."

"We met at one of those stodgy dinners my father's always having," Matt said. "We've been chums ever since. Look where she is now." He

37

pushed Alex from behind so that Alex could see around the corner onto Embassy Row.

Almost all the embassies in Cairo were on this street. Each building was like a fortress, with a tall stone wall surrounding it.

Rachel stood in front of the German embassy. A Nazi flag flew above it, and five German staff cars were parked in front, as well as the motorcycle Alex had seen at the airport. Two guards with machine guns leaned against a staff car, talking casually. They overlooked Rachel, who pretended to sell dates. She glanced at Alex and caught his eye.

Matthew yanked Alex back around the corner.

"She's spying on the Germans!" Alex said to Matt excitedly. "I knew she'd be up to something like that."

"They don't realize she speaks German," Matt replied. "They think she's a blooming Arab, so they talk about whatever they want, right in front of her. We learn all kinds of useful stuff this way."

"Like what?" Alex said.

"The Italians have found the richest tomb ever, and they've hired your old friend Zorin Ungricht to help them get the gold out."

"Yes, I heard," Alex said.

"Of course you did," Matt said. "Rachel learned about it by spying on the Germans, and she told her father. He told his superiors in the French Foreign Legion; then they related the tale to the president of Egypt, who whispered it into the ear of my father, who sent a dispatch to Winston Churchill, who contacted your father." Matt took a deep breath and added, "Rachel and I thought it was a marvelously clever way to get you back here! She's very chuffed about it, you know."

Alex grinned. It was just like his friends to come up with such a good plan.

Rachel came around the corner balancing the tray of dates on her head as if she were a real Egyptian. In Arabic she said, "Excuse me, benevolent sir. Would you care for some sweet dates—fruit of the desert?"

"Rachel!" Alex said with a smile. He gave her a hug. It had been only three months since he'd seen her last, but it felt like longer.

Matt asked, "Did you know you're supposed to be at my place for dinner? We'd better hurry. Our parents will be waiting."

The mention of food reminded Alex that he was hungry. He'd only had a cold beef sandwich on the plane.

"Good idea," he replied. At that moment, he heard a motorcycle engine revving. It was the German he'd seen at the airport!

Alex ducked his head and whispered to Rachel, "Sell me some dates." He didn't want to be spotted with his friends. Rachel looked surprised but began to bring her platter down.

The motorcycle careened around the corner and whipped past them. Alex sighed in relief, but suddenly the driver hit the brakes and did a U-turn. He stopped his bike just inches from Alex and his friends and stared levelly at them.

"I knew there were holes in our security. Now I see how the word leaked out." The German spy smiled grimly. "Fortunately, I am very good at plugging leaks."

"Run!" Alex said, and grabbed the platter full of dates from Rachel. It was made of thick Egyptian clay, baked in a kiln. Alex hurled it like a discus as Matt and Rachel took off running away from Embassy Row.

The spy was just drawing a gun when the plate hit his hand. The gun went spinning into the gutter. The spy whirled to look for it, but Irani's shadow suddenly appeared and stretched out to cover the gun. Thanks to her shadow and the dim light, the spy couldn't see his weapon. He let out a curse and gunned the engine of his bike.

Alex sprinted toward Rachel and Matt. Cairo was an old city, and many of its streets and alleys were just wide enough to lead a donkey through. He knew that Matt and Rachel were running for the market district, hoping to lose the spy there.

The motorcycle engine growled, and Alex heard the bike racing up behind him. Matt and Rachel dodged into an alley. Alex knew it was a dead end.

Alex dropped to his hands and knees behind a merchant's rickety wooden stall. He looked for something, anything, to use as a weapon. He was hoping for a club or a big rock. The only thing on the ground nearby was a pile of rotten grapefruits.

Alex grabbed one in each hand.

The motorbike went zipping past and began to turn into the alley where Matt and Rachel were hiding. Alex couldn't let the spy get them.

He leapt up and hurled the grapefruit with all his might. It hit the front wheel with a *splat*. The wheel wobbled, and the driver lost control.

The motorbike crashed into the stone wall and skidded a dozen yards along the lane. The spy was thrown head over heels.

Alex stood for half a second in shock. He imagined that the driver would be badly injured, but the bike had hardly stopped skidding before the spy managed to climb to his feet.

Matt and Rachel came blasting around the corner like a cyclone.

"Run for it!" Matt screamed.

The spy got to his feet.

Alex threw his second grapefruit and hit the fellow square in the face, knocking him down.

Matt followed Rachel and Alex around a corner, and they leapt a low wall into a little garden in someone's backyard. They squatted for a moment between two bushes.

The spy came rushing around the corner. "I know you're in there," he muttered angrily. "It's only a matter of time before I find you."

Alex could see the top of the spy's head over the stone wall. He was getting closer.

Alex desperately hoped that the man wouldn't see them. He kept perfectly silent. The small bushes offered some cover, but not enough to hide them well.

Beside Alex, Matt began to shake and point to his nose. Rachel glared and clamped her hand over his mouth just as he let out a muffled *"Aaachoo!"*

"Now you're mine!" The spy laughed cruelly and began to climb over the wall.

7

THE WORLD'S WORST LIAR

Alex, Rachel, and Matt stared at each other in terror. Suddenly, Irani's shadow rose up from the ground and wrapped itself around them like a blanket. The spy squinted into the darkness but could not spot Alex and his friends hiding practically in plain sight.

"No!" the spy roared in frustration. He took off, limping, down the street. Irani slowly faded into the night.

"Criminy!" Matt whispered. "That was close!"

Rachel nodded. "What was that?" she asked, looking quizzically at Alex.

"Irani!" Alex answered. "She's one of the mummies from Cleopatra's tomb. Her spirit is trapped here."

Matt's mouth fell open. "Wh-why did she help us?"

Alex shrugged. "She's a friend. She helps us—and we help her find her way home."

Matt shook his head. "If that's what they call friends in London, remind me never to move there."

Rachel's eyes twinkled. "Alex, any friend of yours is a friend of mine. Now come on, let's go!"

Alex grinned. He and Rachel had seen mummies and rotted ghouls of all shapes and sizes. He'd known she would understand about Irani.

They rushed down the street and into the British embassy. Alex's parents still hadn't arrived. As Alex and Rachel followed Matt into Lord Harrill's office, the ambassador glanced up from his piles of paperwork. Matt's father was a distinguished-looking man with thin white hair and a grandfatherly air. He was always trying to free a tourist from jail or decide whether to grant someone's request for a visa to visit England.

"Matt, there you are," he said. "Been looking all over for you."

He was intently reading some official document as he said this, and he seemed so absorbed that Alex felt sure he hadn't been looking for Matt at all but had only been *thinking* in his absent way about looking for him.

"Having a big to-do tonight, you know. Dinner and all that rubbish. You'll need clean socks. Mustn't come to the table without clean socks."

Alex and Rachel tried not to laugh. Matt's dad believed that clean socks were essential for any social gathering. He never mentioned the need for clean shirts or clean trousers.

"I just pulled some on, Father," Matt lied in a quavering voice, as if he might faint from the effort. He was the worst liar Alex knew.

"Good show," Matt's dad said absently. "Dinner will be served shortly. I trust you had a pleasant day?"

Alex looked hopefully at Matt, fearing that he would spill his guts and they would all get in trouble for spying on the Germans. Matt's legs began to tremble.

"It was a truly adventurous day," he mumbled.

His father pushed his glasses up on his nose and peered at the document on his desk. "Honestly," he muttered. "How am I supposed to read this hand-writing? What in the devil are they even requisition-ing? A gross of *frogs*?"

Alex pulled on Matt's elbow, urging him to leave. Rachel cracked the door, and it squeaked. "An adventurous day?" Matt's dad asked. "How so?"

Sweat began streaming down Matt's brow.

"A German spy chased us," Matt blurted out. "Alex beaned him with a grapefruit and ruined his motorcycle."

Matt's dad squinted at his requisition form. "Well . . . that does sound exciting," he said distractedly. "Remember: dinner shortly, clean socks."

As soon as they got out, Alex asked Matt in disbelief, " 'Alex beaned him with a grapefruit'? I sure hope the fate of the world never hangs on your ability to keep a secret."

"I don't think he believed me," Matt said, looking truly relieved. "He thinks I'm playing make-believe."

Alex and Rachel rolled their eyes.

Alex's parents were already seated in the Great Hall talking animatedly with Captain Bronson and

Rachel's dad, Colonel Stroeker. Alex's mum patted the chair beside her and gestured for him to join them.

Matt's dad came down moments later. The Great Hall was decorated to look like a castle. There were real suits of armor standing beside a fireplace that was never used and shields on the wall with the Harrills' royal crest—a bloodred dragon on a white field.

As soon as the dinner was over, Matt's dad sat back in his chair and looked meaningfully at Alex's dad. "Perhaps the adults should retire to my office for conversation." He turned to Matt. "Why don't you take your friends to the parlor? Perhaps they would like to listen to the phonograph."

"But, Lord Harrill—'' Alex began to say.

Matt grabbed his arm. "That sounds perfect," he said, pulling Alex and Rachel down the hall.

"I don't want to listen to the phonograph," Alex said. "You didn't even put up a fight."

"I know," Matt whispered, "but you must see what I've got in the parlor. Trust me."

He rushed over to the sofa, climbed up, and took down the picture of King George.

Alex was astonished. There were three tiny holes in the wall.

Matt smiled proudly and said, "Have a look. I drilled them for just such an occasion."

8
THE DEBATE

Alex peered through his spy hole into the office. His parents sat on a big sofa. Captain Bronson stood stiffly in a corner while Rachel's dad studied a display of old swords that hung on the wall. Matt's dad cleared his throat and looked anxiously around the room.

"Thank you all for coming," he said. "I'll get right to the point. If this tomb has as much gold in it as Evelyn believes, Mussolini must not get his hands on it. The fate of England—and the world—may rest on our shoulders."

"I'm used to that," Alex's dad said knowingly.

"We'll have to leave soon," Rachel's dad said. "Ungricht left the Italian embassy this afternoon, leading a small unit of men to the tomb."

"How small?" Captain Bronson asked.

"Twenty men. They're armed with machine guns, including two fifty-five-caliber guns on tripod mounts. They also have enough dynamite to blow the entire tomb."

"Blow the tomb?" Alex's mum cried. "Good gracious, why would they do that?"

Alex bit his lip. *What about Irani?* he thought. *How can we save her if they destroy her home?*

"Our sources tell us that the Italians have not yet discovered the treasure room—only the antechambers," Rachel's dad answered. "The dynamite will be used to knock holes through walls, in an effort to locate the gold."

"Thank goodness they haven't found it yet," Alex's mum replied. "They can't have disturbed the site too much. We'll have to get to the tomb before Ungricht has his way. How long ago did you say he left?"

"About three hours ago," Matt's dad replied.

"Three hours?" Alex's mum stood up and began to pace. "That's a pretty good lead."

Alex's dad nodded. "Where are they going? What roads will they take?"

Rachel's dad whipped a map out of his pocket. "They'll be at these coordinates, 29.95 degrees east by 28.2 degrees north."

"That's not far," Alex whispered to his friends. "Only a hundred miles. Matt, get some paper from the desk and write down those coordinates."

"Why?" Matt asked. "You're not thinking what I think you're thinking? Because I really don't want to get caught between a bunch of mummies and a unit of tomb raiders."

"They won't let me," Alex answered. "We'll have to leave this one to the adults."

"That's a relief," Matt replied.

Matt went to the desk and wrote down the coordinates. As he did, the adults studied the map.

"That puts them out near Al W_h_t al Bar_yah," Alex's mum said. She traced a path with her finger. "The only road near there is pretty bad."

"Perhaps we could cut straight across here," Bronson said, pointing at the map, "over the dunes?"

"Trucks would never make it," Alex's dad replied. "They'd bog down in the sand. I know a faster way, but it's risky."

"How is that?" Rachel's dad asked.

"We fly."

Matt's dad looked doubtful. "Where would you land? There isn't a runway for miles."

"We land in the sand," Alex's dad replied. "If we leave the landing gear up, we can skid in like a sled."

Matt's dad's face began to flush. "That sounds awfully dangerous!"

Alex's dad shot back, "It's a lot less dangerous than trying to dodge machine-gun fire!"

Rachel's dad patted Alex's dad on the back. "You may have something here."

"You're both blooming nuts," Captain Bronson said. "I won't ask it of my men."

Matt's dad raised his hand to silence him. "O'Connell was asked to lead this expedition. If he thinks it will work, then it's our job to follow him."

"Then it's settled?" Alex's dad asked, looking around the room for approval. Everyone nodded reluctantly. "Let's load up."

Matt's dad went to the liquor cabinet. "Perhaps I could interest you in some of my private stock," he said, and pulled open a cabinet filled with dusty bottles of wine lying in rows. Alex thought perhaps he was going to propose a toast. Instead he hit a switch, and the racks of bottles swung out, revealing a secret cabinet hidden behind the liquor. There were dozens of weapons inside—grenades, rifles, sawed-off shotguns, machine guns—everything they'd need to defend themselves.

Alex's dad threw a rifle to Stroeker and began strapping on a pistol.

Alex's mum wrinkled her brow. "All these guns and dynamite worry me," she said. "We must remember to preserve the archaeological integrity of this site."

"You take care of the site," Alex's dad said, deadpan. "I'll take care of the Italians." He chambered a round in his machine gun.

9

THE SWEETEST CAMEL
IN CAIRO

When the adults came out of the office, Alex, Rachel, and Matt were flopped on the sofa listening to some scratched-up old record.

Rachel's father said goodbye to her, speaking softly in German. To Alex's astonishment, Rachel fought back tears. At the temple of the Scorpion King, Ungricht had staked her out in the hot sun on a bed of scorpions, and she hadn't cried once.

"Alex," his mum said, "we'll be leaving now." Her face was tight with fear, but she tried to sound confident. "We should be back in a couple of days. If there are any problems, call the embassy. And please, try not to get into any trouble."

"Don't worry about me, Mum. I'll be fine."

She gave him a hug. His dad ruffled his hair and said, "Be good."

"Right." Matt's father shook Matt's hand and strode out, leading the adults to the airport.

Alex followed them to the door and looked out, his mind whirling. He wanted to help his parents, but how could he from Cairo?

"You're worried, aren't you?" Matt asked.

"Yes," Alex admitted.

"Want to play cards?" Matt suggested. "It will take your mind off things."

"Who can play cards at a time like this?" Alex answered.

Matt shrugged sheepishly and put the cards back in his pocket.

"I know what would cheer you up," Rachel told Alex. "We can visit Stinkwad!"

Stinkwad was Alex's special camel, trained by the Medjai to bite and kick in defense of his master. Alex had loaned the animal to her when he had moved back to England. Of all the camels in the Sahara, Alex was certain Stinkwad was the fastest— and the smelliest.

"Sure," Alex said, brightening up. They walked to the French embassy's stables, five doors down from Matt's house. The air was crisp and a million stars salted the sky. Stinkwad was in a corral off by himself, but as soon as Alex saw him, he knew that something was terribly wrong.

Stinkwad had gotten fat! It was as if the camel had hardly been ridden at all.

Alex's mouth dropped open. "What did you do to him?"

"Doesn't he look so much better?" Rachel smiled. "We've been feeding him grain with his hay and giving him plenty of rest. Now he's fattening right up."

"But—" Alex leaned in closer and wrinkled his nose. A sweet smell seemed to be coming from Stinkwad's hair. "Is that . . . perfume?"

"He smelled so bad that no one wanted him around," Rachel explained defensively. "The ambassador's wife ordered us to bathe him in rosewater once a week. Even that didn't help much, so she started mixing in just a little perfume."

A little? Alex thought. *He reeks of it.*

Stinkwad was probably the slowest and sweetest-smelling camel within a thousand miles. *He's not my camel anymore,* Alex realized with a sinking heart.

Just then, Stinkwad opened his mouth and gave Alex's cheek a slobbery lick.

"Blech!" Matt exclaimed.

But Alex didn't mind. He knew it was camel-speak for "Welcome home."

"Stinkwad might be different, but he's still the best camel in all Egypt."

Rachel beamed.

Suddenly, headlights shone on the back of the stable. A familiar girl's shadow was in the middle of the yellow light. It waved excitedly, pointing to the street.

"Irani," Rachel said in awe.

Alex got a bad feeling in the pit of his stomach.

Irani was trying to warn him about something. He heard gears grinding as a large truck down-shifted. There weren't many trucks in Cairo. Most people still rode camels and horses. Alex climbed up on the corral fence and looked out at the street.

Within seconds, two trucks rounded the corner onto Embassy Row. A steady stream of trucks followed closely behind.

"What do you see?" Rachel asked.

"Army trucks, with canvas tops," Alex said. In moments he counted twenty, all lining up in front of one of the embassies. Rachel and Matt climbed up next to him.

"What do you think they're doing?" Matt wondered aloud.

"It looks like the whole Italian Army has landed," Rachel said.

Soldiers began to climb from the backs of the trucks. Two pulled the canvas tarp off one truck, revealing an enormous antiaircraft gun. Leaders from the embassy came out to admire the weapon.

"Blimey," Matt said, "there must be two or three hundred troops over there."

A shiver crawled down Alex's spine. Mussolini had gathered more Italian troops to support Ungricht. His mum and dad wouldn't be able to hold out against the reinforcements.

Rachel moaned. "We have to warn our parents!"

"Come on!" Alex said. He leapt into the corral and ordered Stinkwad to his knees. The camel obeyed hesitantly, and Alex quickly threw on a halter and saddle. He climbed on, followed by Rachel and Matt.

Within moments they had the camel up and were

racing out on Embassy Row. The streets were well lit with gas lamps, and the idling trucks made it even brighter. Stinkwad's hooves beat rhythmically on the hard road.

Just as they rode past the German embassy, Alex heard a familiar voice shout behind them, "Halt!"

He looked back to see a large man rushing out of the front gates. It was Ungricht's spy!

The big German soldier ran to a waiting motorcycle, kicked the starter, and came racing after them. His headlight shone on their backs.

"Run, Stinkwad!" Alex shouted. "Run!"

10
STINKWAD TO THE RESCUE

Stinkwad ran as well as he was able. The fat camel grunted and wheezed with every step, moving with all the grace of a charging walrus.

"Halt!" the German spy shouted again. "Halt, or I'll shoot!"

"Faster, Stinkwad!" Rachel cried as Matt dug his heels into Stinkwad's ribs.

Stinkwad panted frantically and tried to charge faster, but Alex knew it was no use. Stinkwad hadn't run in months, and he'd never run with so much fat and so many people on him. The spy sped up behind them on the motorcycle and honked his horn.

Stinkwad was so nervous, he began to poop.

"Good show, Stinkwad!" Matt cried. "Bombs away!"

Alex and Rachel looked back nervously. The motorcycle veered right and left on the narrow road as the spy tried to avoid the flying camel dung, but the bike still moved just as quickly as before.

"He's gaining on us!" Rachel warned.

Alex looked ahead and saw a shadow running next to the camel. Irani was with them!

She pointed left, down a narrow street. Alex veered, so that only Irani's shadow was now on the road. She stood in front of the motorcycle, waving her hands for the driver to stop.

"Aaagh!" the spy shouted. He swerved to avoid the shadowy woman, and his motorbike slid into a wall with a *thud*.

There was no time to lose. Alex kept going, urging Stinkwad to the airport as fast as the camel could go. By the time they got there, poor old Stinkwad was pooped out in more ways than one.

But the airport was closed, and the plane was already gone.

11

AIRMAIL

"How can we get a message to them?" Rachel asked as they looked out over the empty airport.

"Maybe we could take a car and race through the night," Matt said.

"No," Rachel said. "It would be too slow. Besides, we wouldn't want to run into Ungricht's convoy."

"I know," Alex told them, "Izzy!"

"What's an Izzy?" Rachel asked in bewilderment, as if it were a new word she hadn't learned.

"He's not a what, he's a who," Alex said. "Izzy's a friend of my father. He has a zeppelin!"

"A zeppelin?" Rachel asked. "Isn't that some kind of blimp?"

"Yes," Alex said, "it's great!" Four years ago, Izzy had carried Alex's family away from the Scorpion King's temple to safety in his zeppelin. Alex had seen Izzy a couple of times since then. His old airship was ratty-looking and patched in dozens of places, but it would fly, and Izzy had made some special upgrades.

"Well . . . ," Matt said slowly. Alex knew what he was thinking. Matt was afraid of just about everything—especially heights.

"Wells are for wishing," Alex said. "Come on. Izzy will take us. This will be fun!"

"I suppose it would be faster than a camel . . . ," Matt admitted.

"Come on," Alex urged again. "Let's go!"

Izzy lived dozens of blocks away, out on the edge of the desert in a ramshackle hut that was so dumpy, it looked as if it belonged in a junkyard. His blimp was tied out back among the weeds and old wheelbarrows. It loomed above the house, making everything look tiny in comparison.

Alex pounded on the door. Light from an oil lamp shone through the front window, and Alex peered in. The lamp sat on the table with some dirty dishes and a crusty milk bottle. There was no sign of Izzy.

"What a bother," Matt said, peering over Alex's shoulder. "He's not here."

"He's not," Alex ventured, "but his blimp is."

Rachel began jiggling the old-fashioned drop latch on the front door, trying to get into the house.

"We can't just take it!" Matt said in astonishment.

"Not if we can't get to it, that is," Rachel said.

"We'd just borrow it for a bit," Alex argued. "I know how to fly it. Izzy would understand. There are lives at stake."

Matt began to twist his sleeve nervously. "Maybe we should go back home," he proposed. "Our parents said to stay out of trouble. My father would give me such a scolding if I took off with you."

"We can't help it if trouble found us," Alex said.

Rachel nodded. "You can go home if you want— and miss out on the fun."

Matt bit his lower lip. Alex could see the wheels turning in his head. He was imagining what it would be like to go home and play solitaire or, worse, challenge himself to another game of chess. Rachel was still trying to get the door open.

"Oh, criminy! Try this," Matt finally said, and banged the doorjamb just above the latch. The door swung open with a creak.

12

A SHIP IN THE DESERT

Alex didn't tell his friends, but Izzy's zeppelin was not the safest vehicle. The rubber-coated cloth on the outside of the balloon was patched in eight places. A decrepit old fishing trawler hung from the balloon with an airplane propeller sticking out of the back. The propeller engines looked as if they were held together by rust.

Then, of course, there were Izzy's modifications—crude rocket engines hidden at the back of the trawler.

"This thing flies?" Rachel asked.

"Yes," Alex said, "and if we have to make a crash landing on water, it even floats!"

Matt stared at Alex in horror. "We won't crash, though, right?"

Alex simply winked. "Rachel, make sure there's

plenty of gas and oil in the engine." He climbed into the fishing trawler for the preflight check. It was a mess. A few crates served as tables and chairs, and bags of sand lay on the floor. There was a dirty plate heaped with dried-out chicken bones sitting on the motor. Alex tossed it away and put the lantern in its place.

Izzy had taught him that the zeppelin's huge balloon was actually made up of a cluster of small balloons. Each one was called a cell. Alex checked the gas pressure gauges by the motor and found that cells two, five, and nine were all low, so he manned the hydrogen pump and filled two and nine. Even after he pumped hydrogen into cell number five for several minutes, the needle on the gauge didn't move.

Alex groaned. Either the gauge was broken or the cell had a hole in it. *Probably both*, he figured. *It better not slow us down.*

Matt and Rachel got the engines running.

"Alex," Matt asked, "what are all these bags of sand doing hanging over the edge of the boat?"

"They're called ballast," Alex said. "They hold

the zeppelin down. If you ever want to gain altitude, you just empty them or throw them off. If you want to lower the ship, you just let a little gas out."

Alex quickly checked to make sure the ship's compass worked. He took Matt and Rachel and showed them two levers. "This handle is the rudder," he explained, twisting the left one. "It lets you turn the ship right and left. This one here is the elevator. If we have the engine running, it tilts the ship up or down, so that we can pull up or dive down."

When Alex felt pretty sure that Izzy's zeppelin might work, Rachel climbed to the ground and untied the ropes that were holding it down. As she loosened each tie, the zeppelin bucked and lurched a little higher into the air. When she yanked the knot free on the last rope, the zeppelin seemed to leap into the sky.

"Alex!" Rachel called out. The zeppelin had lunged so quickly that it was leaving her behind.

Alex heaved a rope ladder over the side of the fishing trawler. "Grab it!" he called.

Rachel leapt for it and missed. She ran along the ground, trying to keep up with the drifting zeppelin, jumping up after the rope. The zeppelin was floating too high. "I can't get it," she called. The zeppelin rose higher. "Alex!"

"What are we going to do?" Matt cried, running in circles in panic.

Alex fumbled with the elevator, trying to lower the zeppelin. It was no use. The motors weren't going yet, and the zeppelin continued to drift. Just as Alex was afraid Rachel would never catch up, the blimp dipped in the wind and she managed to catch the last rung of the ladder in her fingertips.

She fumbled to hold on as the zeppelin began to soar higher. "Help me!" she grunted, her arms shaking under the strain.

"I'm coming!" Alex replied, and scampered down the ladder as far as he could.

"Oh, dear," Matt cried. "If you slip, you'll both break open like melons!"

"Thanks for the helpful advice, Matt," Alex muttered, and leaned further down. He grabbed Rachel by the collar of her dress and held on with all his might.

They were floating hundreds of feet above the desert, the night wind blowing in their faces.

"You know," he grunted, "it would really be rather pleasant here if we weren't in danger of dying."

"Pull me up a little higher," Rachel grumbled back, "and maybe I'll enjoy the view a little more."

Alex took a deep breath and managed to pull Rachel up a yard. As soon as she got her feet on a rung, she was able to climb.

Alex crawled back into the fishing trawler and dropped to the floor. He lay panting and sweating. A moment later, Rachel fell beside him.

"Are you two satisfied?" Matt asked, shaking his head. "You could have fallen, and then what would I have done?"

Alex looked up and grinned. "Missed us? Now, be a good pal and fire up the engines like I showed you."

"I ought to turn this thing around, that's what I ought to do," Matt muttered to himself, but he did as Alex asked.

Alex stood up and looked out. The air was so still that it felt as if the heavens were holding their breath. The zeppelin rose two hundred feet, and then Matt used the elevators to keep them at the same altitude.

There was nothing in the sky besides the zeppelin and a million stars—no clouds, no moon, no birds. Alex mopped the sweat from his forehead with the back of his shirtsleeve.

Rachel stood up next to him. "Look, a fire!" she said, pointing below them. Dull red light reflected from a column of smoke several miles to the north. "Shall we go have a look?"

"It's too dangerous," Alex warned, then added reluctantly, "Izzy's zeppelin leaks like a sieve. There's hydrogen gas hissing out of the cells all over the place. If even the smallest spark touches that gas . . ."

"What?" Matt asked nervously.

"Kaboom!" Alex answered.

"Oh, dear," Matt said, his eyes growing wide.

"Don't worry," Alex told him. "We'd be barbecued by the time we hit the ground. Besides, if you've got to die, you might as well go out in a blaze of flaming glory."

Rachel groaned. "I knew you were going to say something like that."

Alex squinted into the night. He could barely see the line of the dirt highway that led south gleaming in the starlight below them.

"Follow that road," Alex told Matt.

Matt opened the throttle. The propeller sounded like a squeaky door, and Matt fretted, "Could there be a bat caught in the engine?"

"Nah," Alex answered. "It always sounds that way."

A soft wind blew in Alex's face. He figured they were making about fifteen miles per hour. *Is that fast enough to warn our parents in time?* he wondered.

By now they should have crash-landed the plane and perhaps already made it to Cleopatra's tomb. Hopefully, they were still safe. . . .

He tried to imagine their surprise when the zeppelin touched down in front of them and Alex stepped off with his friends. He imagined warning them of the danger, and how grateful they would all be when he gave them a ride home to safety.

The zeppelin crossed a rocky ridge, and Alex saw a campfire, several tents, and some trucks two hundred feet below. A thin man in a long black robe leaned on a walking stick near the campfire.

"Ungricht," Alex whispered as a chill crept down his back.

Rachel's face turned pale. "Turn! Turn!" she warned Matt.

Matt grabbed a handle on the control board and pushed down. The zeppelin lurched into a dive—straight toward the camp!

Ungricht shouted a warning. Three Italian soldiers stood guard beside the trucks. They raised their rifles. Smoke issued from their gun barrels, followed by the *plunk, plunk, plunk* of bullets striking the balloon.

"Aaagh!" Matt screamed.

"Pull up!" Alex shouted. He dove for the control panel and grabbed the elevator stick, bringing the zeppelin out of its dive. Hair rose on the back of his neck as more bullets struck the balloon. He could hear hydrogen hissing from it. Only dumb luck kept the gas from igniting, turning the zeppelin into a huge bomb.

Alex fumbled for the afterburner switch that would light Izzy's special rockets. He hit the switch.

There were a *hiss* and a *whoosh* as the rockets ignited.

"Whoa!" Matt screamed as the zeppelin lurched forward. He clung to the sides of the fishing trawler to keep from being thrown overboard. But as quickly as the thrusters had fired, they died!

"What's wrong?" Rachel shouted. Alex hit the ignition switch again and again.

"The rockets must be out of fuel!" Alex cried.

"We're dropping fast!" Matt warned.

Alex wrenched a rudder, turning the balloon to the right, desperately trying to get out of range of the Italians' guns.

He read the gauges. The gas pressure was dropping in cells one through six, all across the front of the zeppelin. When those emptied, the balloon would nosedive into the desert. Ungricht and his men would catch them easily.

Alex jammed the elevator switch to full so that the zeppelin would climb as high as possible.

"Throw over the ballast!" he shouted. "All of it! We're going to crash!"

Bullets plunked against the metal floor of the fishing trawler under Alex's feet. The zeppelin was right over the Italians' camp.

Rachel began hurling sandbags over the side,

hoping to boost the zeppelin higher in the air. Each bag landed with a *whomp*, like the sound of a cannonball striking the ground. A scream rose from below as a sandbag struck a guard.

"Got one!" Rachel shouted in relief. "Matt, throw something on Ungricht!"

She grabbed another bag off the floor and hurled it overboard.

Matt gleefully began tossing out anything at hand—a dirty plate, a heavy wrench, one of Izzy's old boots. He grabbed a rickety old box and was about to toss it, too.

"Don't throw that out!" Alex warned. "That's Izzy's repair kit."

"Sorry," Matt said, and grabbed a crate. Alex noticed a sign on the bottom: WARNING—DYNAMITE!

"Not that either!" Alex shouted, but it was too late. The box went over.

Three seconds later there was a tremendous *boom!*

A cloud of dust, smoke, and flames rose up, threatening to engulf the zeppelin. The guns went silent for a moment as the Italians began shouting and rushing around.

Please work, please work, Alex prayed as he hit the thrusters again.

They slowly came back to life with a groan, easing the zeppelin away from Ungricht's camp. Alex checked the gauges for the gas cells. The needles on two, three, and five showed empty. Three of the other fourteen cells were leaking hydrogen.

"Keep throwing out anything we don't need!" Alex told Matt and Rachel. "It's only a matter of time before we crash."

1 3
THE ESCAPE

Alex's mouth felt dry. Nervous sweat dotted his forehead. The zeppelin was going down. There was nothing he could do to stop it—except try to keep it from crashing near Ungricht.

"Rachel, help me with the heavy stuff," Matt called. He went into the bottom of the fishing trawler and began lugging up the mattress.

Even with almost all the ballast gone, the zeppelin wasn't rising the way it should. Alex had to do something more.

He grabbed some greasy rags by the engine and scampered up the lines to the balloon. It was like climbing the rigging of a ship. He searched desperately for bullet holes, with nothing but starlight to guide him. He didn't dare take a lamp near the gas leaks for fear that a spark would blow up the whole blimp.

He squinted desperately in the darkness, but it was no use. The holes were too small to see. His hands began to shake.

Suddenly, he saw the faint shimmer of a girl's shadow.

"Irani?" he whispered. "Is that you?"

A dim finger pointed to a tiny spot on the balloon. Alex rushed up the guide wires and stuffed a greasy rag into the bullet hole. When he finished, he peered about again. The shadow pointed to another hole, and another, and another.

Alex smiled gratefully. "Thank you, Irani," he whispered into the night air. The shadow seemed to nod, and then just as quickly as it had appeared, it was gone. Alex sighed and climbed back into the trawler.

Matt and Rachel had thrown the sandbags and just about everything else overboard, until there was barely anything left.

"Alex," Matt called. "Do you still want the toolbox?"

"No," Alex said with regret.

There was a clank as the toolbox went over.

"Do you want this radio?" Rachel asked.

"No," Alex replied. There was a rattle as it went over the edge.

Rachel shook her head. "We're going to have to pay this Izzy person back when we get home," she said. "I won't get another allowance for as long as I live."

Matt gulped and clutched a shiny pair of binoculars to his chest. "I—I think we've thrown enough supplies overboard," he said, and gently placed the binoculars back on the shelf.

Alex felt the zeppelin level off and then begin its slow descent. With any luck, it would keep traveling for a few hours before it crashed. To the east, he could see the faintest light gleaming on the horizon.

He looked back north. Ungricht's camp was several miles away, but Alex saw something that made his palms begin to sweat: headlights, piercing the darkness.

"Oh, no," he whispered. "Ungricht is following us."

1 4
THE CRASH

The headlights followed the zeppelin until a rose-colored sun drifted above the horizon. As the trucks followed, the airship kept sinking closer to the ground. The way the early-morning shadows filled the wind-swept dunes made Alex imagine the waves of the sea.

All through the night, they had steered a course toward the oasis at Al W_h_t al Bar_yah, near Cleopatra's hidden tomb. As they approached the area where it should be, Alex warned Matt and Rachel, "Keep your eyes open. We should be close."

"Do you mind if I shut my eyes for a second when we crash?" Matt joked.

Rachel ignored him. "Let's each focus our search. Matt, you look east. I'll look west. Alex, you look ahead."

"Good idea," Alex said. He scanned the dunes

but saw no sign of their parents' plane or Cleopatra's tomb.

To make matters worse, there was no oasis anywhere in sight. When the zeppelin went down, there would be no water to drink, no food to eat, no hope of rescue.

Alex's head began to throb as he realized how foolish he had been. He'd wanted to warn his parents, but everything was going wrong.

Soon the zeppelin dropped so low that the fishing trawler barely skimmed the tops of the dunes. At any moment it would crash. Alex hoped for a gentle landing in the sand.

"Irani," he whispered. "I know you're out there somewhere. You showed me the spy and the bullet holes. I promise that if you show me the way to the tomb, I'll do everything I can to help you find peace."

He searched for some sign of Irani's shadow, but for once she seemed to have deserted him.

Alex turned off the engines, slowing the zeppelin so that only the morning wind carried them. As they neared a hill of sand, he called, "Hang on to something. This could get rough."

"Too bad we don't have more ballast," Rachel said.

"Alex," Matt teased, "you're the one who got us into this mess. Why don't you be a brave lad and throw yourself overboard?"

Alex narrowed his eyes. "If you don't be quiet, we'll throw *you* overboard."

They skimmed a dune, dropping so close that the bottom of the fishing trawler skimmed the sand. For a hundredth of a second the airship paused; then the wind drove them on. The next dune loomed ahead.

"Hold on!" Alex shouted.

The front lip of the fishing trawler plowed into the sand. Overhead, struts screamed in protest and then snapped.

The sudden jolt threw Alex out. Sand sprayed in his eyes as he rolled head over heels down a dune with Rachel beside him. He came to rest on his back with his head pointing toward the base of the dune and started counting bruises. *One on my left shin, two on my right arm, three on my—*

Wham! Rachel slammed into his back, and Alex felt another bump forming.

"Thanks," he muttered. "I needed that."

Rachel rolled over and glared at him. "The next time I fall out of a blimp, I'll try to aim better."

"Help!" Matt's scream cut through the desert.

Alex and Rachel looked up. The zeppelin was still flying overhead, carried like a leaf in the wind, but the trawler had broken halfway off. It was upside down and Matt's shoe was caught in a fishnet.

He drifted forty feet above the sand as the fishing trawler neared the next dune. If Matt didn't get out soon, Alex was sure he would be squashed like a bug.

"Hurry, Matt!" Alex called.

"Jump!" Rachel shouted.

Matt kept wriggling, trying to get free, until his shoe suddenly came off and he fell facedown on the sand with a groan. The fishing trawler hit the top of the next dune and snapped off of the balloon completely. Released from the weight of the trawler, the balloon rose in the air again and blew away.

"Matt?" Rachel cried, but he didn't answer.

Alex climbed to his feet and began loping down the dune to his friend. The sand was thick and deep, making it hard to run.

Alex reached Matt and flipped him over. "Matt, Matt, are you okay?"

Matt had sand and grit ground into his face, but no broken bones or bleeding.

Impossible, Alex thought in shock, until he saw a shadow cradling Matt's body like a net. Alex breathed a sigh of relief as Irani's shadow wiggled out from beneath Matt and shimmered in the hot orange sun.

Matt gasped, spit some sand out of his mouth, and squinted up at Alex. "Is this heaven?" he asked groggily. "Are you an angel?"

"Sorry to disappoint you," Alex told Matt, "but this isn't heaven. This is where people fry."

15

WALKING WITH THE DEAD

A lex, Rachel, and Matt rummaged through the wreckage of the zeppelin, looking for anything that might be of help. There wasn't much. They'd thrown over all the sandbags and tools in the dark, trying to keep the zeppelin airborne. If there had been any food in one of those crates, it had been tossed out hours ago.

They did have three canteens full of old water and some very stale biscuits. These were Izzy's emergency rations, and it was hardly enough to last a day. Beyond that, they had no weapons and no extra clothing for protection from the sun.

"Well, that's it," Matt said as he piled the booty at their feet.

"Three canteens, some biscuits, a pair of binoculars, and a flashlight?" Rachel asked. "How are we supposed to live on that?"

Matt licked his lips. "If we were in Cairo right now, we'd be having fresh bread and marmalade."

"Thanks for reminding me," Alex replied as his stomach began to growl. "Let's start walking."

He handed Matt and Rachel each a canteen, put the flashlight in his pocket, and strung the binoculars around his neck.

"Which way should we go?" Matt asked.

"Anywhere but here," Alex answered.

He climbed to the top of the nearest dune and looked out over the sand in every direction.

"We've got to be close to the tomb," Rachel said hopefully.

Alex couldn't see any sign of it, but just as he was about to give up, Irani's shadow beckoned them to the east. "That way," he said with a grin.

They walked for half an hour, following Irani's wriggling shadow across the dunes, slogging through a sea of sand. Sweat poured off Alex, and his canteen was almost empty.

The more they walked, the more he worried about his parents. Irani's shadow would lead them to the tomb, but what would they find when they got there?

He looked back at Rachel. Her face was pinched with a frown.

"Is that gunfire?" she asked. "Do you hear shooting?"

Alex listened intently, stilling his breathing. "I don't hear anything."

She nodded grimly. "My imagination, I suppose. By now, the battle is probably over—"

"Yes," Alex said. *I only hope our parents won.* He massaged his cramped legs and hurried on.

Thirty minutes later, Irani's shadow pointed toward the horizon and then faded into the sand. A mile away, gold shimmered in the morning sun.

"Is that it?" Matt asked excitedly.

Alex peered through the binoculars and saw an ancient Greek temple on top of a pyramid in the distance. Fluted white columns supported a gold roof.

"Yes!" Alex replied. "Cleopatra was one of the last pharaohs, but her family was from Greece. She combined Greek and Egyptian traditions—and built a temple over her tomb. This has to be it!"

Alex could see a dozen men toiling outside the tomb with shovels, trying to clear sand away. A couple of tents were pitched close by, and near them stood a pair of trucks.

The men wore drab gray uniforms. Italian soldiers!

"Everyone down!" Alex said. He dropped to the sand and pulled Rachel and Matt down with him.

"What's going on?" Matt asked.

"The Italians still have control of the tomb," Alex answered. "We can't let the soldiers see us."

"You mean our parents aren't here yet?" Rachel asked.

Alex peered through the binoculars again, looking for signs of a battle. There were none, just a couple of muscular soldiers carrying a gold-covered coffin.

Alex dropped the binoculars and peered hesitantly at his friends. He wasn't sure if he should be relieved that his parents were still alive or worried about why they had never made it here.

"Maybe they couldn't find the place," Matt offered. "It would be hard to spot in the dark. Maybe they're still wandering in the desert."

"That must be it," Rachel replied. "They're probably still wandering in the desert somewhere."

Alex nodded, but he had a sinking feeling in his gut. He was afraid something had gone terribly wrong.

No, he told himself. *They're still coming. They just got delayed somehow.*

Matt took a small sip from his canteen, paused as if he might take another, then prudently put the cap back on.

"What now?" he asked.

Alex's head was whirling. They were trapped in the desert. The sun was already blistering hot. The only food, water, and shelter were ahead of them, but Ungricht and his men were about to reach the site, and reinforcements would follow soon after.

"What do you think?" he asked Matt and Rachel. "It looks like maybe eight or nine soldiers up there."

"There might be fifty more in the tomb," Rachel warned.

Alex knew they had only one choice. They could lie out here in the sun and bake, or they could try to take Cleopatra's tomb from the soldiers right now.

He thought of all the gold inside the tomb and how it would help finance Mussolini's war. He thought about the code of the Medjai and how he had sworn to protect the tombs at all costs. He thought about his promise to Irani to help her find peace in the afterlife.

Really, Alex had no choice at all.

16
THE TOMB

"**W**e have to get into the tomb," Alex said.

"You're bonkers!" Matt said. "There's no way!"

Alex paused thoughtfully as he remembered the story his mum had told him.

"What is it?" Rachel asked eagerly.

"Long ago," Alex began, "Cleopatra and her husband, Mark Anthony, tried to escape the Roman legions. Cairo was under siege, and its defenses were rapidly crumbling. Cleopatra planned to commit suicide rather than admit defeat. She had all her treasure gathered together into a hiding place, then came here to inspect her tomb."

"I know that story," Rachel said. "We're reading Shakespeare's play about it in my advanced English class at school. Mark Anthony returned from the battlefront and asked a servant where Cleopatra was. She told him, 'She is in her tomb.' "

Alex nodded. His mum always got teary-eyed when she got to this part.

Rachel continued. "Mark Anthony thought she meant that Cleopatra was already dead, so he drew his sword and stabbed himself in the stomach. He couldn't bear to live without her.

"When his servants found him dying, they put him on a chariot and rushed him to see his wife one last time. Cleopatra held Mark Anthony until he died, and afterward she went mad with grief." Rachel shook her head. "What a mess."

Alex agreed. "To make matters worse," he added, "some of Octavio's men had followed Mark Anthony to Cleopatra's tomb. Her guards blocked the front entrance, but Octavio's men snuck around to the back. They found a small window there and managed to climb inside."

"Yes," Rachel said, her eyes glowing. "After they caught Cleopatra, they planned to kill her in Rome. Instead, a servant brought her a bowl of fruit with an asp hidden inside. Cleopatra held the snake to her chest and let it bite her to death."

"Good show!" Matt said. "Can you imagine that, letting a snake bite you on purpose!"

"That's not the point of the story, you ninny," Alex said. "The point is: there's a back way into the tomb—a window!"

"Right," Matt said. "I knew that. What I want to know is, if Octavio's men caught Cleopatra in her tomb, then how come she's still there with her treasure?"

"Egyptian priests saved her," Alex answered. "They believed that their queen was a goddess and that it was sacrilege for her body to be taken back to Rome. They stole Cleopatra's corpse and brought it back with all her treasure, so that she could be properly buried." Alex paused and looked directly at Matt. "The Medjai say Octavio searched for months for it, but he went back to Rome empty-handed."

"Amazing," Matt whispered, and looked expectantly at the tomb.

The Italian soldiers were digging at the front, trying to find their way down to the treasure room.

Alex knew from his mum that they were looking in the wrong place. Unlike most pyramids, where the treasure room was hidden underground, in Greek temples like Cleopatra's it had to be near the top.

He heard the distant whine of engines. Trucks were coming across the desert—Ungricht and his men!

"Come on," Alex said. "We'll have to circle around to the back."

They took off at a jog and ducked over the dunes behind the ruins. When they were certain no guards were coming, they crept quietly up to the pyramid.

The base of the temple was still buried in sand. Only a dozen massive columns peeked above the dunes, holding the roof. It was decorated with a magnificent gold frieze that showed Hercules fighting a seven-headed serpent.

"Where would the window be?" Rachel asked Alex.

He studied the frieze and the columns, looking for some sign of an entrance. "Look," he said, pointing to two columns. The creamy white stone had a trace of gray soot lodged in the crevices, as if it had been damaged in a fire. "Irani's coffin was covered in soot, too."

Alex went to the spot and began to dig, pulling

the sand back by armfuls. Matt and Rachel went to work beside him, widening the hole.

They had dug only four feet before Rachel said, "I think I found it."

She scraped away some sand to reveal a small stone square with bits of plaster flaking off it.

Alex chipped at the plaster and uncovered a crude adobe brick. "It looks like they tried to cover up the air vent with cheap white plaster to make it look like the surrounding stone," he whispered. "Here, give me some room."

Rachel and Matt crawled away from the hole. It took only a couple of good kicks to knock down the bricks. They fell in with a *clank*.

Alex hesitated. The hole below him was dark. He could smell the rancid, papery scent of mummies and the dust that had piled up in the tomb over the ages. It was an odor that brought back foul memories, but he had to stop the Italians from plundering the tomb. And he had to keep his promise to Irani.

Alex slid through the tiny air vent and down a long chute, into the treasure room of Cleopatra's tomb.

17

CLEOPATRA'S TREASURE

Alex landed lightly on his feet and stood still for a moment. A small beam of sunlight came through the hole up above, barely illuminating the room.

Alex pulled out his flashlight, and for the first time in two thousand years, light shone upon Cleopatra's treasure. Gold was everywhere—on platters and spoons, vases and canopic jars, and statues of the gods Isis, Anubis, and Hathor. There were shields, spears, beds, and chairs for the queen to use in the afterlife.

Treasure was heaped on every bit of the floor and leaned against every wall. Alex stared in awe, his jaw dropping.

The room was enormous. Alex guessed it was more than three hundred feet long, two hundred feet wide, and eight feet high. The shaft of light coming in from the window illuminated the mounds of treasure nearby, but most of it was hidden in the darkness. Even with his flashlight, Alex couldn't take it all in. He could only make out the forms of more wondrous things in the shadows—chariots, furnishings, and coffins galore.

"What do you see?" Matt called.

Alex hardly knew where to begin. He was sure that no tomb of an ancient king had ever held such treasures—not even King Tutankhamen's. "Nothing much," he mumbled.

"Oh, criminy," Matt groaned. Seconds later he slid through the air vent and fell to the floor. He climbed to his feet and began to dust off his trousers, then looked up and gasped.

Alex waited for him to say something, but Matt was speechless.

"Watch out below," Rachel called. Alex grabbed Matt and yanked him out of harm's way just as Rachel came through the vent.

She landed in a crouch, like a cat, then stood looking at all the gold. A little coughing noise was all she could manage.

"Don't touch anything," Alex warned them.

"What do you mean, 'Don't touch anything'?" Matt said, his mouth watering greedily.

"The gold. Don't touch it."

"Come on, Alex," Matt protested. "It's not all yours. It should be *ours*—a three-way split."

"No," Alex said. "It's cursed."

"Are you sure?" Rachel asked, stepping closer.

"Mummy's gold is always cursed," Alex said. "The Medjai taught me that. It's meant for the pharaohs to spend in the afterlife."

"What will happen if I touch it?" Matt insisted.

"My dad told me about a boy who went blind," Alex replied.

Matt stared at the gold, eyes wide, and murmured, "That wouldn't be so bad, would it? Blind, but fabulously wealthy—"

"That's not the worst of it," Alex said. "The boy went blind because maggots ate his eyes. It took them a week to gnaw their way out, and then they bored into his brain. He met a bad end."

At that moment, a strange groaning sound filled the room, as if one of the mummies was talking in its sleep.

Matt stood up straight as a board, his eyes nearly popping from his head. "Well," he said soberly, "let that be a lesson to us all, then."

Alex could tell that Matt was cowed for the moment, but he didn't know how long it would last. "Come on," Alex said. "Let's look around."

"Look for what?" Matt asked.

"Irani will show us," Alex said confidently.

A shadow appeared in the beam of his flashlight and began to take a winding path through the treasure, walking past piles of golden necklaces and headdresses, climbing over a golden harp. Alex followed for fifty feet, until Irani's shadow stopped short and pointed up.

"She's pointing toward the ship!" Rachel said.

The ship's deck had burned away long ago, and the ribs of the hull were mostly charred cinders, but Alex could see the gold leaf near the floor. Two of the masts had burned, but one was only partly damaged. It leaned over like a blackened finger, still trailing shreds of purple silk. A few blackened silver oars sat in the oarlocks. The ruined ship was tragic and majestic.

"Here's the source of your fire!" Rachel said.

"Yes," Alex replied in amazement. He was sure it was the very same ship in which Cleopatra had been sailing down the Nile when she met Mark Anthony. *She must have brought it to her tomb so they could sail on it together in the afterlife,* he realized.

His eyes lit up. Suddenly, everything made sense. "The Egyptians believed that in order to reach heaven, they had to sail through the waters of hell. Otherwise, they'd be eaten by sea monsters. Octavio knew they needed a ship!

"He must have burned it and doomed her spirit to wander the earth—along with the spirits of all the servants in Cleopatra's court, including Irani."

As if to emphasize the point, Irani's shadow suddenly faded from view.

"Where did your friend go?" Rachel asked.

"She's showed us what she needs," Alex said. "Now it's up to us to get her a new ship."

"Alex," Matt asked in a quavering voice. "All these coffins lined up against the wall—do you think any of them are . . . occupied?"

"Yes," Alex said, smiling. "I think *all* of them are occupied."

"R-right," Matt stammered, his eyes growing wider with fear. "Just checking."

"Let's look for the door," Alex said, leading the way.

The tomb was huge, and Alex had to pick his way through a tangled mess. There were combs made of fish bones covered in gold, a spinning wheel, bolts of silk, and golden masks inlaid with ebony and azurite.

They reached the far left wall after several minutes and looked up at the writing on the wall. Some of the hieroglyphs were covered in soot and hard to read, but Alex could make out most of the ominous words. "Death unto all who violate this sanctum," he read to Rachel and Matt. "May dark Anubis lead them to their tombs, and may the crocodile-headed goddess gnaw upon their hearts of greed. A curse I pronounce upon Rome, upon those who would rob the pharaoh. If any man of Rome touch the forbidden treasure, death shall come upon Rome's armies. If any of her people touch the forbidden gold, the Dark God of the Underworld shall swallow their king. . . ."

Matt shuddered. "I—I think maybe we should go back now—"

"Not yet," Rachel replied.

Alex nodded. "We still need to find Cleopatra's coffin."

Suddenly, they heard deep voices growling in Italian by the entrance.

Matt panicked and shouted, "Help! They're on to us!"

Flashlight beams cut through the darkened room. Alex dropped to the floor, but Rachel shrieked and took off, leaping over a pile of treasure. The flashlights swung around, pinning Matt in their glare.

He was frozen in fear.

Rachel reached the air vent and leapt up, vainly trying to climb out of the tomb.

Flashlight beams shone on her, and someone shouted, "Halt!" A warning shot bounced off the wall above her head.

Rachel stopped and stood with her hands against the wall.

Alex scampered behind a golden couch. He heard more soldiers enter the treasure room, searching.

Flashlight beams lit the walls above him. He had to find a place to hide.

Desperately, he glanced right and left. He spotted a large golden casket. Without a second thought, he cracked the lid and crawled in to lie down with the dead.

18

THE COFFIN

Alex lay upon a papery mummy, its sharp bones poking through its bandages. The air inside the coffin was stale and carried only the tiniest scent of rot. Alex heard the deep *thud, thud, thud* of a beating heart. He tried to calm himself, but the steady hammering continued.

Outside the coffin, voices grumbled not far away. Though the lid to the casket was covered with gold leaf, the wood inside had long since decayed. Pinpricks of light shone through tiny holes and cracks. Alex twisted on the old bones and peered out into the treasure room.

Ungricht strode into the room, followed by a lieutenant with a disfigured face. He looked as if he'd suffered a severe burn that had left scars where there should have been flesh. Alex fought back a shudder.

The guards pinned Rachel's and Matt's arms behind their backs and pushed them forward.

"Let me go!" Matt shouted. "Let me go!"

Rachel struggled silently to get free, but there were too many soldiers, and they were too strong.

Ungricht held up his ebony walking stick as if he might strike them.

"So," he said to Matt and Rachel, "you were the children in the zeppelin. I knew you would come."

"You had better let me go!" Matt commanded in a high, terrified voice. He looked at the stick in Ungricht's hand and stammered, "My—my father is a diplomat. I have diplomatic immunity!"

"There is no diplomatic immunity from death," Ungricht said, and laughed coldly. He reached up and stroked Rachel's cheek.

"We meet again," he told her. "I know your name now, Rachel Stroeker. Where is your little friend Alex?"

"Dead," Rachel lied. "Your men shot him last night, in the zeppelin."

Ungricht glared at her. "I don't like your tone, young lady. You did not learn to fear me at the

Scorpion King's temple, but you will do so now. I must devise an especially painful death for you."

"If you don't set us free, you'll be in big trouble," Matt declared.

"How so?" Ungricht said. "Do you imagine that someone will come to save you? No one will come. Our spies made sure of that. The plane your parents sought to fly here never took off. It blew apart two miles down the runway, and all aboard were killed. That ended their pathetic attempt to reach the tomb before me."

Alex's heart pounded in his chest, and he felt as if he couldn't breathe. *Blown apart? All aboard killed?* He remembered seeing the flames in Cairo, and he felt sure that Ungricht was telling at least a partial truth. But there was something else in Ungricht's tone—fear.

"You're lying to me," Rachel said, her eyes narrowing. "I can see it in your face. You're lying. You know my father will come, and you're afraid of him."

Ungricht laughed menacingly and told the guards, "Take them into the hallway. There is an old pit there with some bones at the bottom. Lower them down, pour lantern oil on them, and let it soak in. When we are ready to leave, we will throw torches on them."

He laughed again and peered all around, as if searching for something.

Me, Alex thought with certainty. *He's looking for me.* Slowly, Ungricht's eyes scanned the room. He squinted at the coffin where Alex lay and then looked beyond it.

"Take the gold!" he shouted to the guards. "Load it all onto the trucks, quickly! I'll search the rest of the tomb for the boy."

Ungricht strode out of the room. The scarred lieutenant picked up a golden goblet, admired it for a moment, then put it in his bag and left the room. The guards wrestled Matt and Rachel out after them.

Alex had never felt so alone. His heart kept racing, and he gasped for air. He had no backup, no weapons. He wasn't sure if his parents were alive or dead. He knew only one thing—he couldn't let Ungricht kill his friends.

"A true Medjai never gives in to fear," he recalled Ardeth Bay telling him once, "and you are on your way to becoming a Medjai."

Alex gritted his teeth. "I have a job to do," he whispered. The blood was no longer rushing through his veins, and his breath came easier.

He could still hear a heart beating loudly in the coffin. Alex listened closely, then gasped. It was coming from the mummy he was lying on!

I'm not alone at all, he realized.

He remembered how Irani's shadow had led him to the tomb and protected him from harm. Even if he couldn't save the gold from the Italians, he had to keep the promise he'd made to her!

THE WAILING OF LOST SOULS

Alex glanced through the holes of the coffin. There were looters in the treasure room, brawny soldiers with guns and grim faces, grabbing whatever looked most valuable. One man palmed a golden dagger. Another picked up an earring and hid it under his tongue. Every one of them was out for all the treasure he could steal.

As the men neared, Alex took a deep breath and shoved the lid of the coffin open.

"Santa Maria!" one of the closest soldiers shouted, and fired his gun in the air. Two others fainted outright.

They think I'm a mummy, Alex realized. He laughed and raised his arms as if to surrender.

Two guards trained their weapons on him and began shouting, apparently ordering him to step out of the coffin. They were trembling with fear, and

Alex worried that one of them might accidentally pull the trigger.

Alex stared at them calmly and began speaking in ancient Egyptian. "Cleopatra, Mark Anthony," he called. "I hope you can hear me. I need your help if I am to set you free."

Instantly, there was a rustling sound, like invisible feet shuffling through fallen leaves. A deep groan came from inside the coffins.

The guards stared at Alex in horror, as if aware of what he had just done. Alex felt majestic and powerful. He held his breath, knowing that the dead would rise.

The rustling grew louder as spirits rushed into the room from every direction, hissing through the corridors and through chinks in the rocks.

Frightening shadows began to flit across the walls. There were priests bearing spears and wearing the jackal-headed mask of Anubis. There were grim warriors carrying ancient Egyptian swords.

The Italian soldiers began to scream in terror. One of the guards raised his rifle and took aim at a fleeting shadow. He fired, and Alex heard a death scream as the bullet bounced off the wall and struck the guard in his chest.

Suddenly, all the soldiers began shooting. Bullets flew across the room, bounced from walls, and rebounded. Two more guards screamed and fell.

Alex ducked for cover and listened to the moaning of ancient Egyptian sorcerers. "Come," they seemed to whisper. "Come, and we shall show you to the lake of fire! Come, and we shall show you where the madmen cry."

All along the walls, coffins that had been bolted closed for centuries suddenly exploded open. Mummies staggered from their graves, mummies wrapped in gray linen, with rotting holes for eyes and naked yellow teeth. Mummies with dried fingers, perfumed with the stench of decay.

The Italian soldiers reeled back in horror and began firing weapons into the mummies. Bullets exploded dry skulls and shattered the mummies' chests, but the mummies outnumbered the guards a hundred to one. When one fell, ten others took its place. They carried thick swords and battleaxes. They rushed into the fray with no fear of death, roaring battle cries that had not been heard in a thousand years.

Alex thought that the soldiers would surely retreat, but he underestimated the depth of their greed and their resourcefulness.

A dozen more soldiers raced into the treasure room, followed by Ungricht. They formed a solid wall in front of him and fired boldly into the crowd. Mummies charged but were cut in half as they neared.

Keening wails arose. Alex had never heard a sound quite like it. It was the death cry of shadows.

"Irani!" Alex cried, for he feared that her shadow was among them.

A LEADER OF ROME

"We will not be defeated!" a voice seemed to call in ancient Egyptian from high above the fray.

Alex looked up in relief. Standing in a casket on the ruins of the golden ship was a powerful ghoul with a golden shield and dagger. His face had rotted away, leaving only a naked skull, but something about his regal posture commanded respect and fear. Alex almost felt as if he should drop to his knees.

He knew instantly that it was Mark Anthony. In his own country he had been a commander of the Roman legions, the largest army his world had ever known. In Egypt, he had been more than a king—he had been worshipped as a god.

"Follow me!" Mark Anthony cried to the mummies. He pointed his sword at Ungricht. A thousand voices gave an answering shout. The mummies charged toward Ungricht, swinging their ancient swords fiercely.

The Italian guards were suddenly struck with terror. They tightened their circle around Ungricht, raised their machine guns, and fired into the mass of charging mummies.

Some mummies were blasted into bits of dry flesh, but others kept charging. Even the mummies that were blown in half kept crawling toward the tomb raiders as best they could. Mark Anthony strode boldly toward the soldiers, shield raised high. Alex saw bullets sparking as they bounced off the golden armor and dropped uselessly to the floor.

A click echoed across the room as one of the guards tried to fire an empty chamber. He was out of bullets. Almost instantly, another guard did the same, and a third. Fear filled their faces, for the mummies kept charging. One by one, each of the guards ran out of ammunition, and the mummies gained ground.

Ungricht knew he was doomed. He glanced

around the room, searching for Alex. "I shall have my vengeance upon you—and your friends!"

He turned and raced from the tomb, fleeing the mummies, his black robes fluttering like raven wings behind him.

THE PIT

As the mummies hacked at the remaining guards, a new fear filled Alex. Ungricht had promised vengeance, and his men still had Rachel and Matt!

Alex raced for the door of the tomb, following Ungricht over treasure and past mummies. He grabbed a golden sword from a dead Egyptian priest for defense.

Ungricht ran two hundred feet, then slammed a stone door closed behind him. Alex shoved it open with all his might and raced down the hallway, looking for the pit that held his friends. Almost every pyramid he had seen had some sort of pit near the treasure room—it served as a trap for would-be tomb raiders.

Alex rounded a corner and aimed his flashlight down the hall. A nervous Italian man stood there in plain clothes. Alex was sure he was just a truck driver, not a trained soldier. The man's legs and hands were shaking as he dumped the contents of a gas can into a pit that spread nearly from wall to wall. He was so frightened that he was spilling gas everywhere—into the pit, on the walls, on his pants.

At the sight of Alex's sword, the man yelped in terror and threw the gas can into the pit.

"No!" Alex warned. "Don't do it!"

The man flicked the lighter, preparing to burn Alex's friends to death. The lighter sparked and a steady flame rose. He backed away, mumbling in choppy English, "S-stay back. Don't touch me!"

"Look," Alex said. He threw down his sword. "I'm not armed."

The man was trembling with every step. He glanced into the pit, then back up at Alex. He seemed to be afraid of more than just mummies. Alex suspected he was frightened of Ungricht.

"Don't do it!" Alex begged again.

The fellow crossed himself. He threw the lighter, but he was shaking so badly that it didn't land in the pit. Instead, it landed at his feet.

Instantly, the gasoline caught fire and enveloped the man's legs. He screamed in pain and retreated down the corridor, beating at the flames.

Alex stared at him in horror, then ran to the edge of the pit. Luckily, the fire hadn't reached it. Alex aimed his flashlight down and called out, "Are you all right?"

Rachel and Matt were crouching on the floor, their clothes soaked with gasoline.

"We've been better," Rachel replied, shivering. "Can you get us out of here?"

The smell of gasoline rising from the pit was overwhelming. Alex could hardly stand the fumes. If he didn't get them out quickly, his friends might suffocate. Alex looked around frantically, then saw a rope coiled nearby.

He wrapped one end of the rope around his wrist and tossed the other end into the pit. "Climb up!" he shouted. He braced himself, hoping he would be strong enough to help them. Rachel grabbed hold of the rope and began pulling herself hand over hand out of the deep pit.

"You're almost there," Alex told her. His legs had started to quiver, and the rope was sliding slowly through his sweaty palms. Even if he could get Rachel out, he doubted he would have any energy left for Matt.

Suddenly, a loud roar echoed off the walls behind him.

Mark Anthony's ghoul was rushing toward him, leading an army of mummies. He stopped short in front of Alex and pointed at him with his sword. "*Khentu*," he murmured, his tone full of respect. Alex knew the word meant more than "friend." It meant "chief among my friends" or "my closest friend."

Alex felt his face flush with pride. "Yes, *khentu*," he repeated.

Mark Anthony gave a curt nod, then grabbed the end of the rope. Other mummies lined up behind him, and together they pulled Matt and Rachel to safety.

THE CURSE

Matt stared at the ghoul of Mark Anthony and opened and closed his mouth in shock, unable to frame words.

Rachel looked at the fierce warriors and managed a weak "Thank you."

"You are welcome," Mark Anthony replied in ancient Egyptian. Then he and his mummy guards charged down the corridor.

"Come on!" Alex shouted to Matt and Rachel, and ran to keep up.

The sunlight outside was blinding. All the Italians' trucks still sat downhill, only fifty yards away—all but one. A jeep was speeding from the tomb across the desert.

The driver was the scarred Italian lieutenant. Ungricht sat beside him.

Mark Anthony raised his sword and shouted to his troops in ancient Egyptian.

"What's he saying?" Matt asked.

Alex translated the howling words as best as he could. " 'Go now, I command you! Hunt these jackals to the ends of the earth, and bring back our treasure!' "

Alex felt troubled by Mark Anthony's orders. He both feared and hated Ungricht, but the mummies deserved to be at peace. Besides, there were larger issues at stake.

"Please, no!" Alex begged.

Mark Anthony turned and gazed at him as if to ask his reason.

"The gold of the tomb is cursed to any man of Rome who steals it, right?" Alex asked.

Mark Anthony nodded.

"Those two men stole little, only a goblet. A greater evil has risen in modern-day Rome, a powerful man named Mussolini who hopes to rule the earth. The man who took the goblet is his agent."

Mark Anthony smiled and clapped Alex on the shoulder. "You are wise, friend, for one so young.

The raiders may have their golden goblet—and the curse that follows it. Mussolini's armies cannot win. He himself will die a miserable death."

Alex gazed at the retreating jeep. For months now, he had been following the news of Hitler and Mussolini and worrying about the coming war. He hoped the curse would still work after so long. But he knew that Hitler and Mussolini were dangerous men who might cause enormous harm before they were defeated.

23
REUNIONS

Alex, Rachel, and Matt stood at the foot of the temple with the mummy soldiers and watched the jeep retreat until it was no more than a speck on the horizon.

Suddenly, a murmuring came from behind Alex as the mummies voiced their respect. Cleopatra was stepping from her tomb.

She stood between two white columns of the Greek temple, with the ornate golden roof gleaming above. She wore an ancient headdress decorated with lapis lazuli and a silk dress that shone bluer than the sky.

She was the most regal person Alex had ever seen, but he stared at her in puzzlement.

Why didn't she rise during the battle? he wondered. Then he thought of how she had first appeared to

Mark Anthony on her splendid boat, and suddenly it was clear to him.

"She always did know how to make an entrance," he whispered to Rachel.

Every mummy soldier fell to one knee before her, but Mark Anthony strode up the steps and took her hand.

At that moment, Alex heard a familiar voice call, "Alex? Alex? Is that you?"

He turned and looked behind him. His mum and dad were standing on a nearby sand dune, along with Matt's and Rachel's dads, Captain Bronson, and twenty of England's finest soldiers. Irani's mummy was leading them.

"Mum! Dad!" Alex called, and rushed toward them with Rachel and Matt close behind. They each threw their arms around their parents and hugged them tight. Words could not express the relief Alex felt. He'd half believed Ungricht's lie about their deaths.

"What in the world are you doing here?" his dad finally asked, looking back and forth between Alex, Matt, Rachel, and the mummies.

"We came to warn you that Mussolini is sending

more reinforcements," Rachel answered hurriedly. "We were afraid they'd be here by now."

Rachel's dad shook his head. "The embassy heard about the troops and cut them off just outside Cairo," he said reassuringly. "Thanks to you and your friends, the tomb is safe now."

Matt looked pointedly at his father. "That's good news, but what took you so long?"

His father blushed and looked at the sand. "We got lost."

Alex's mum nodded. "Even when you know where this place is supposed to be, it's a devil of a hard spot to find. The only reason we managed is because Irani appeared in the desert an hour ago and guided us."

Irani smiled modestly and shrugged.

That must have been when her shadow disappeared in the tomb, Alex thought. He clasped Irani's papery hand in his own. "You are a true friend," he said.

His mum reached out for Irani's other hand and stared at the two mummies behind Alex.

"Mum, Dad, I'd like you to meet two more friends, Anthony and Cleopatra."

24

HEAVEN'S SHIP

A few minutes later, Alex and his mum sat on the steps of the temple, listening carefully to Cleopatra. Her words were distant and muffled, but somehow they could understand them.

"We have waited in my tomb long, but there is no ship to carry our souls to heaven." She stared off into the desert, her voice full of pain. "Octavio burned all my ships."

"I heard," Alex's mum said sympathetically.

Alex wished there were something he could do. *The only thing I have is Izzy's—* His eyes lit up. "I know where there's a ship!" he said.

Cleopatra and his mum looked at him in surprise.

"It's a sky ship," Alex hurried. "I flew here on it."

"Of course!" his mum replied. "Izzy's zeppelin!"

"Is it near?" Cleopatra asked.

"Not far," Alex said. "It's only about an hour's walk away!"

Cleopatra clapped her hands in surprise, and within moments Alex, Rachel, and Matt were heading across the desert in a truck with their parents and the mummies.

Matt kept looking up at his father as if he couldn't quite believe he was still alive. "Ungricht told us you were dead," he said, choking on his words. "He said there was a plane wreck in Cairo."

Matt's father shook his head angrily. "What a cruel man to tell such lies," he said. "There *was* a wreck, but it was a plane full of Nazi officials who went down. Surely Ungricht knew the truth."

Alex looked out over the rolling dunes, and part of him wished he had let Mark Anthony's mummy guards chase after Ungricht. *Next time*, he thought, *we won't let him get away.*

Moments later, they reached the site of the wreck.

Izzy's old fishing trawler was not nearly as fancy as Cleopatra's golden ship, but Mark Anthony inspected it and assured Alex that it would work.

They used ropes to tie the fishing trawler to the

bumper of a truck, then towed it like a sled back to the temple. Mummy soldiers picked the fishing trawler up and carried it to the steps.

There the ancient mummy priests said prayers over it, consecrating it for its journey to heaven. By evening it would be ready.

As Alex waited for the priests, Captain Bronson came to him with a backpack. Inside was a military radio with a hand-cranked battery. "I've made my report," he said. "But there's someone on the radio who would like to congratulate you."

"There is?" Alex asked in surprise.

Bronson nodded.

Alex picked up the receiver. "Hello?"

A crackling sound came from the other end of the radio, and then he heard, "Winston Churchill here. Alex, I understand that you are to be commended. You did a fine job. If you ever need a favor, anything at all, I hope you'll feel free to call on me."

"Uh, thank you, sir," Alex said, flustered.

"It all sounds rather frightening," Churchill added, "between the mummies and the shadows."

Alex shrugged. "It wasn't so bad—especially when I thought about how much was at stake."

"You're a smart lad!" Churchill chortled. "Always remember, we must never give in."

After Alex finished the call, Irani's mummy walked shyly up to him. "You have been a great help, Alex," she said. "I bring you an offering in thanks."

She held out a fabulous golden headdress in the shape of the falcon god Horus, with blazing blue eyes and shimmering wings. "It is a small gift, I know," she said modestly, "not nearly as rare as a ship in the desert."

Alex gazed at it in awe. It was a valuable gift—valuable enough to repay Izzy for his zeppelin and have money left over. Even more important, it was a gift of gratitude, and Alex was honored to receive it.

"It's perfect," he said gratefully. "Thank you—for everything. Your name shall always be remembered fondly."

Night was beginning to fall, and a silver moon had appeared. Irani climbed the steps of the temple and entered the tomb. She waved her hand and closed the door gently behind her.

As soon as she did, a cold wind rushed through the pillars of the temple. Sand blew up from the desert, swirling fiercely around Alex and his friends.

They all backed away, racing for the shelter of the trucks. Alex squeezed into the front seat of a truck with his parents and stared into the rearview mirror as his dad drove a few hundred yards to safety.

The howling wind heaved sand over the top of the pyramid behind them. Alex knew it would be hidden by dawn.

Suddenly, a brilliant red light pierced the night. In his heart, Alex felt sure that Cleopatra, Anthony, and Irani had found peace.

ABOUT ANCIENT EGYPT

CLEOPATRA VII

Cleopatra VII became queen of Egypt in 51 B.C., when she was a mere eighteen years old. Egyptian law forbade women to reign without a male co-ruler, so she married her brother, twelve-year-old Ptolemy XIII. After a power struggle, Ptolemy banished Cleopatra from Egypt, and she did not return until she befriended Julius Caesar, ruler of Rome. Ptolemy XIII died soon thereafter, and Cleopatra married another brother, Ptolemy XIV, and returned to power.

Cleopatra was actually a Macedonian, but she ruled as an Egyptian and was beloved by her subjects. In 333 B.C., Alexander the Great, from Macedonia in northern Greece, conquered Egypt and freed the Egyptians from the Persians, who had controlled Egypt since 525 B.C. The Egyptians were grateful to him for this and revered him as a pharaoh. After Alexander's death in 323 B.C., just before his thirty-third birthday, Ptolemy, one of his powerful generals, became king of Egypt. Generations of Ptolemaic kings and queens ruled Egypt from 323 B.C. through 30 B.C. Cleopatra was the last ruler of the Ptolemaic dynasty. She was actually the seventh queen to bear this famous name.

Cleopatra was a very well-educated woman. She spoke nine languages and was knowledgeable in mathematics, astronomy, medicine, music, and art. During her rule, Egypt was under constant threat from the Romans, who wanted to control the rich Nile valley. Cleopatra understood the threat of takeover and wisely befriended the powerful rulers of Rome—first Caesar, then Mark Anthony, who fought by her side at the end of their lives.

When Cleopatra traveled to Tarsus (in present-day Turkey) to meet Mark Anthony for the first time, she wanted to make a strong first impression. She sailed into port on a ship with purple sails and silver oars, dressed as Aphrodite, the Greek goddess of love. Cleopatra's likeness appeared on both Roman and Egyptian coins, a privilege reserved for the most powerful.

Cleopatra inherited a kingdom plagued by war, famine, and drought. During her short lifetime, through her intelligence, diplomacy, and political influence, she nearly restored Egypt to its former glory and health as a nation. But in 31 B.C., the Romans defeated Mark Anthony's troops in a sea battle off the coast of Actium, Greece, ending

Cleopatra's reign and yielding her country to Rome.

THE AFTERLIFE

Egyptians built massive pyramids as graves for their beloved pharaohs. The burial chamber and ante-chambers—offering room after room filled with the pharaohs' treasures—lie deep inside the pyramids and can be reached only by following long, sloping passageways. These passageways were often sealed with thick slabs of granite called portcullises to prevent looting and destruction.

Sarcophagi—the giant outermost stone coffins containing the mummies—were so big that the burial chambers and pyramids were built around them. Several structures surround the giant pyramids, including queens' tombs, which are smaller pyramids, temples, and a boat pit, containing all the boats the pharaoh might need in the afterlife.

Egyptians believed that each person consisted of four parts that would live on after death:

• The *Ka*—a spirit-like copy of a person. The *Ka* wanted and needed all the things humans need—food, water, clothing, and other earthly goods. The *Ka* could leave the body while it was sleeping but always needed to return to survive. The *Ka* was depicted as a human with arms on its head.

• The *Ba*—a person's unique, nonphysical character traits, the personality. The *Ba* was depicted as a human-headed hawk. The *Ba* left the body at death and reunited with the *Ka* to become an *akh*—the form of the person fit for survival in the underworld. Because this reunion was all-important for ensuring passage to the afterlife, Egyptians created well-preserved, highly decorated, easily identifiable mummies and buried the mummies with everything the *Ba* or *Ka* could possibly need.

• The name—Egyptians believed that if a pharaoh's given name was written on the walls of the tomb and was repeated often by the living, the pharaoh would have eternal life.

• The shadow—A person's shadow was inextricably linked with him or her, in this life and the next.

Egyptians decorated the walls of tombs with spells and advice to help their dead navigate through the dangerous underworld and on to the afterlife. Eventually this collections of spells became known as the Book of the Dead. These spells were written in hieroglyphics—Egyptian picture writing.

The Opening of the Mouth ceremony prepared

the mummy to eat, drink, speak, and move in the afterlife. Priests used particular tools and recited special spells during this ritual, which took place at the entrance to the tomb. The ceremony freed the *Ba* to find its eternal home deep inside the burial chamber with the mummy.

Though they removed most of the internal organs, Egyptians left the hearts inside their mummies. On the journey through the underworld, the gods weighed the heart against the deceased's deeds and determined whether or not the deceased was worthy of eternal life. If not, the Devourer of the Dead would eat the heart, and the deceased would never reach the afterlife.

Some Egyptians were so well preserved by the mummification process that their eyelashes are still intact!

Poor Egyptians were buried in common graves in the desert. While they were not lucky enough to have pyramids built to protect their remains, the desert sands mummified their bodies very effectively, drawing moisture from the bodies, preventing decay.

RECENT DISCOVERIES

In 1996, beneath the sediment and water of the harbor of modern-day Alexandria, a team of underwater explorers discovered the royal quarters of the ancient city of Alexandria, home to Cleopatra and Mark Anthony.

Scientists believe that the royal city was buried deep in the Mediterranean during devastating earthquakes, tidal waves, and landslides in the fourth century.

Statues belonging to Cleopatra's father, the remains of a ship from between 100 B.C. and 130 A.D., and wood from a pier from the fifth century B.C. are just some of the many artifacts scientists have discovered. Based on these remains, archaeologists can determine a great deal about how ancient cities were built, the materials people used, the objects they crafted, the gods they worshipped, and how and when a city was destroyed.

These discoveries are the result of more than a thousand dives and will soon yield an accurate map of an ancient city people have only been able to imagine until now.

ABOUT THE AUTHOR

Dave Wolverton is a *New York Times* bestselling author with thirty-five books to his credit. He has written more than a dozen books for middle-grade readers, including The Mummy Chronicles Book I: *Revenge of the Scorpion King* and the Jedi Apprentice series. He set a new Guinness record for the world's largest book signing on July 3, 1999.

Besides writing books, he has helped design such bestselling video games as StarCraft's Broodwar and Xena: The Talisman of Fate for Nintendo 64, and Runelords for Gameboy. He is currently producing his first short film and teaches science fiction and fantasy writing at Brigham Young University in Provo, Utah.

Dave Wolverton can be reached by e-mail at dwolvert@itsnet.com.